THE Third Side

M. A. Simonetti

M. A. SIMONETTI

There Are Three Sides to Every Story:
Yours, Mine, and the Truth

ISBN: 149350875X
ISBN 13: 9781493508754
Library of Congress Control Number: 2013920074

CreateSpace Independent Publishing Platform
North Charleston, South Carolina

In Loving Memory of Margaret Simonetti
1917 (?) to 1997

Acknowledgements

I am grateful for the love and support I received during the writing of this book. Many thanks to my editor extraordinaire, Claudette Sutherland, for her encouragement and her red pen. Jan Grazer and Doris Schoenecker are my loyal readers and good enough friends to be honest with me. Lalo and Charlie Bruhl poured the wine on the night we decided on the murder weapon- equal thanks for the vino and the idea. Dr. Steve Schoenecker gave me sound medical information which I then applied as I saw fit- mea culpa's are mine, not his. Speaking of mea culpa's- thanks go to Sue Buske for finding the typos. Pat Scott purchased the right to have a character named after her- thanks to Pat for supporting the charities of the Mercer Island Women's Club. For the record, the real Pat Scott is every bit as intelligent and beautiful as the fictional Pat Scott, but a whole lot younger. Love and Hugs to my Darling Son, Anthony Simonetti, for the marketing advice. As always, none of this would be possible without my very own Patron of the Arts- my Wonderful Husband- Marty Simonetti.

Lo vi amo tutti!

Chapter One

My four o'clock appointment was late, and that did not sit well with me. Lloyd Evans had agreed that we would meet at his office at four. It was now 4:03, and he was nowhere in sight.

"Mr. Evans is five minutes away, Mrs. Fox."

This came from the blonde receptionist after she hung up the phone.

"He asked me to show you to his office and make sure you are comfortable."

She gave me a practiced smile, one intended to assure me that I would be well watched over until Lloyd Evans managed to show up. I considered returning her smile with a snarl to convey my displeasure at his tardiness, but then I remembered Lloyd's nicely stocked liquor cabinet. Perhaps she intended to make me comfortable by pouring me a drink. With that in mind, I agreed to follow her down the hall to Lloyd's office.

As she led the way, I noted she had the requisite long legs to match the blonde hair and the smile. She wore the professional attire that Lloyd demands of his employees—a knee-length black skirt, tailored white blouse, and blonde tresses pulled back into a ponytail—but she accessorized the look by leaving the blouse just a little too undone. That, and the stiletto Louboutins with their sexy red soles, added a dash of "come hither" to her look. I guessed her age to be between twenty-six and thirty. And I wondered where the hell she had come from.

My name is Alana Fox, and I am the gatekeeper to Malibu society. I have lived here for nearly thirty years, ever since my then-husband and I bought our first house and I set about turning his trust fund into a fortune. Twenty years into the marriage, he did an about-face and left me for Little Miss Tight Buns—a twenty-something bimbo with a desire to procreate. The divorce left him with the house. I held on to the friends. Then I used my social clout to ensure Little Miss was never invited to any party, bar mitzvah, or garage sale north of Topanga Canyon.

Worked great—great enough that I created a tidy little business arranging social connections. If you understand the value of a stellar social network, I am your new best friend. Assuming, of course, you are willing to do exactly what I tell you.

I pride myself on knowing everyone in town: the teetotalers and the drunks, the tennis players and the couch potatoes, the artists and the accountants. I know who lives where, who does what, and who does who. So Lloyd Evans's new blonde receptionist bothered me. Her I did not know. And the last time I let a twenty-something blonde run around unsupervised, I lost a husband.

We reached the end of the hall, and the blonde opened the door that guarded Lloyd's inner sanctum. His offices sit on the second floor of the Malibu Town Center, a U-shaped building housing nifty little boutiques on the ground floor and office space on the second floor. Lloyd owns the Town Center complex as well as hundreds just like it all over Southern California. Commercial real estate is not a glamorous business, but you can make a living at it. Lloyd has done better than most. His name is spoken around town in the hushed tones used when speaking of "real money."

"Please have a seat, Mrs. Fox."

Easier said than done if the goal was to make me comfortable. Lloyd's decorating style leans toward eclectic. Meaning the choice for sitting was either a low-slung black-leather chair that would allow me to rest my chin on my knees or a couple of black-and-white cowhide chairs that looked in need of vaccinations.

The blonde noted my apprehension.

"Perhaps you would be more comfortable by the window."

A conversation area sported a couple of sofas and a coffee table under a picture window that looked over the parking lot and across the street to the civic center. The black-leather and cowhide theme continued there, but at least the sofas appeared vermin free.

"Did Lloyd say where he was?" I asked.

"He is coming in from LA on PCH, but with this horrible weather, the traffic is slower than usual."

We both looked out the window at the mention of the weather.

It was indeed horrible. A nasty Pacific storm had its sights set on Malibu. Gray skies and wind preceded rain that was expected to hit the coast that night. The local weather people wore their sad faces when informing viewers of the approaching storm. The weather service already had issued grave warnings regarding mudslides and flooding. In Malibu we take these warnings seriously because there are so few roads in and out of town. The Pacific Coast Highway (PCH) is the main artery, and it has a tendency to get knocked out by mud and rain. Odds were good that Lloyd was stuck in the rush of people either leaving Malibu or trying to get home to Malibu. Odds were even better that he wouldn't arrive within five minutes.

I had plenty of time to get the goods on the blonde. And then snag a drink.

"I don't recall seeing you here before," I said. "How long have you worked for Lloyd?"

She looked startled. "Don't you recognize me, Mrs. Fox? I'm Angie, you know, Teresa and Will's daughter? Mr. Evans is my grandpa."

My turn to be startled. I swear, the last time I saw Lloyd's daughter Teresa, her three little girls were, well, little. "Bobby socks and patent-leather shoes" little. It couldn't have been that long ago. Could it?

She noted my confusion. The kid was good at reading faces; I'll give her that.

"Gramps makes me call him 'Mr. Evans' when we're working."

"That must be it," I said. "What have you been up to since I last saw you?"

Turned out she had been up to a lot. All the things I would expect from an Evans grandkid. High school cheerleader and president of the honor society, college at UCLA on an academic scholarship followed by a couple of years doing good around the world. Currently working part time at Gramps's office while pursuing a PhD in Something Meaningful. I listened enough if not intently. I decided I wouldn't need to supervise her activities around Malibu, but that didn't mean I couldn't use her at some point. That undone shirt and the Louboutins told me she was more than a globe-trotting Mother Teresa. I filed this info away in my mind just as Lloyd Evans's Mercedes sloshed its way into the parking lot.

"I'll run and tell Gramps you are here. I mean, I'll tell Mr. Evans." Angie raced out with a giggle.

Which left me alone to entertain myself. I decided it would be rude to help myself to a drink after trying the liquor cabinet and finding it locked. So I amused myself by debating whether the decor was outdated or fabulous. The cowhide-and-leather thing could go either way. But then there was that god-awful postmodernist painting hanging on the back wall. I shuddered to think how much Lloyd had paid for it. The damn thing looked like someone had taken finger paints to a plate of glass, framed it, then hung it up backward. I turned away before it made me cry.

I approved of the wall of bookshelves. Something about a collection of books lifts my spirits. Lloyd's books looked like they had each been read, cherished, and put away so they easily could be found again. Interspersed among the books were the usual family photos and diplomas. I went closer to see if I could recognize Angie in any of them.

No such luck—the photos were all of Lloyd. Lloyd receiving a trophy. Lloyd holding up an award. Lloyd fishing.

Fishing?

One entire shelf was devoted to displaying old fishing reels and shots of Lloyd standing knee-deep in a river, holding a trout in his bare hands. The last thing I ever expected was to find out that Lloyd Evans, that pillar of elegance and good breeding, was a fisherman. To hire a fleet of fishermen to hunt and gather fish for him, yes. To venture into cold water on his own and catch them by himself? Never.

"Alana, so good to see you! Traffic was a nightmare! How are you?"

Lloyd swept into the room like a burst of bright energy. He is a handsome man even at the age of eighty plus. He has a full head of shiny white hair and an honest grin. He has the means to have his clothes custom made and keeps a butler on staff to shine his gold buttons. Until I noticed the shot of him fishing, I never had seen Lloyd with as much as a scuff anywhere.

"I am well, Lloyd." I gave him a hug.

"Angie tells me you didn't recognize her!" Lloyd said, as he took a seat at his desk. "She has grown up, hasn't she?"

"Yes, she has." I decided my tetanus shot was up to date and sat in one of the cowhide chairs. "I honestly can't remember the last time I saw her."

"Well, let's see," Lloyd said. "Teresa and Will moved out to the Valley when Angie was twelve, so that would have been thirteen years ago. We had a going-away party for them, as I recall. You and Alan were still married then, weren't you?"

"Yes. We had just finished the house." Alan is the ex-husband married to Little Miss Tight Buns. The house sat on a rise overlooking the Pacific Ocean. I had found the lot, negotiated the deal, designed the house, and supervised its building with every intention of never living anywhere else ever again. So much for good intention. Little Miss Tight Buns was now systematically destroying my masterpiece by filling it with children.

I changed the subject.

"I've reviewed the lease agreement," I said. "Everything is in order. I put you down as my reference, by the way."

I signed the lease, and my hand hardly shook at all.

Lloyd signed too, and before you could say, "bankrupt," I was on the hook for five grand a month.

"Shall we toast to our new business arrangement?" Lloyd asked.

Finally a drink. Lloyd pushed a button by his phone to summon Angie.

"Please bring in a bottle of Champagne," he said when she arrived. "Mrs. Fox and I are going to celebrate."

"So tell me, Alana. You have been sitting on this lease for a few months now. What made you decide to move ahead with this?"

"It is the right time," I replied. "I had to get a few things in order before I was ready."

A few things like setting up a proper bank account, dancing through the bureaucratic nonsense to get a business license, then figuring out how to siphon fifty grand in cash into the bank account without alerting the IRS.

My tidy little business was cash only from its inception. I kept the cash neatly deposited in shoeboxes in my guest bedroom so I didn't have to inform the IRS what I was up to. I will admit to being surprised at how much had accumulated there. It wasn't until the money went missing that I acknowledged the advantages of having a bank account. When the money was mostly recovered (that's another story), I told myself I was going to go legit as a business. A business that no longer operated out of my beach house and stored the proceeds in shoeboxes. Which is how I ended up owing Lloyd Evans five grand a month for the foreseeable future.

My brand-new business space was right next door. My lease included a small reception area with a decent-size office overlooking PCH. For all intents and purposes,

I was a legitimate businesswoman. The whole endeavor scared the crap out of me.

Angie appeared with the Champagne then handed me the keys to my new office.

Lloyd opened the bottle with ease, poured two glasses without spilling a bubble, and toasted with "Here's to a long and happy association."

I seconded the motion. The stuff was chilled perfectly. Of course.

"I haven't seen Alan in a while," Lloyd said out of the blue. "I hear he and Tori are expecting again. Is this the third?"

Tori is Little Miss Tight Buns. And yes, she was pregnant. This was the third one. The second one wasn't even a year old.

"Rumor has it. I don't socialize with them." I sounded curt. I meant to be.

Lloyd didn't take the hint.

"I would like to meet with Alan and kick around a few ideas I have."

He hadn't asked a question, so I said nothing. Most people are so eager to fill a conversational void that they will just blurt out the first thing that comes to mind. But Lloyd Evans isn't most people. He settled quietly into enjoying his Champagne while I wondered what the hell he wanted from me.

"The world of real estate certainly has changed, hasn't it?" Lloyd said, as he poured another glass of bubbly. "This economy is killing small businesses. I can't tell you how many empty properties I am holding. How is Fox Real Estate doing?"

Ah, so that was it. A little competitive curiosity. The fortune I built from Alan's trust fund came from a commercial real-estate empire. Fox Realty Trust was a competitor to Lloyd.

"It's tough all over," I agreed. "Alan is hanging in there, but I can't say business is growing."

"Let's hope the worst is over." Lloyd sighed. His face, ever so briefly, betrayed the worry of every business owner in California. The rotten economy, the high taxes, the dearth of public services. The only thing the Golden State had going for it was the weather, and now even that was lousy. I was about to echo his sentiments when a gust of wind shook the walls of windows. Then the lights flickered.

"I'd better get going." I rose from my seat.

"Are you settling in for the night? I am afraid this storm will hit before morning."

"No, I have dinner plans tonight. I am going to Grace McDonald's house for a girls'-night-out thing. And you know what? Her mom will be there. You know Francis Ferguson, don't you?"

"Really."

Lloyd's tone stopped me in my tracks. It held an undercurrent of surprise, as if I'd just told him I was going to walk home barefoot. I turned to face him.

"You sound surprised."

He recovered nicely.

"Oh, no, no. I'm glad Francis feels up to socializing. She and Milton were everything to each other. I just hope she isn't taking on too much too soon."

I didn't have a chance to ask him what he meant.

Another blast of wind hit the building, and this time it took the lights with it.

Chapter Two

MEREDITH

Meredith Mackenzie told herself the chaos before her was nothing more than preholiday madness. Thanksgiving was still ten days away. The real hell was yet to let loose.

Meredith stood in the doorway of Errands, Etc., the errand-running/concierge business she owned that made the lives of Malibu's residents easier. Whether the task was picking up dry cleaning, shuttling the kids to soccer practice, house-sitting, or buying gifts, Meredith's capable staff took care of it all.

The Errands, Etc. office suite took up half of the second floor of the Malibu Town Center. The main room was an open loft that featured a giant whiteboard listing the errands and requests of the day. Open shelving stored everything from wrapping paper and bows to soccer balls. In the middle of the room stood three rows of counters where the staff busily assembled gift baskets. A hallway led to two small offices in the back. One was

Meredith's. The other belonged to the office manager, David Currie.

The ground floor of the Malibu Town Center housed cute little boutiques Meredith didn't have time for and a coffee shop she couldn't live without. She was on her way to get her third espresso of the day.

"I'm going down to Beans. Anyone want something?" This was addressed to the staff in general.

"Darling, it's nearly five o'clock! Aren't you planning on sleeping tonight?" David Currie emerged from his office with a sincere expression of concern. David was a stump of a man. He looked every bit the former Ivy League rugby player he once had been, even in his dapper lime-green tie and pink button-down shirt.

"Yeah, I know, but this rainy weather makes me sleepy," Meredith said.

"All the more reason to stay off the caffeine. We'll all have trouble sleeping tonight with this storm."

David and Meredith looked out the front windows at the same time to see palm trees whipping in the wind. Then they both looked up to the ceiling, where a previous storm had leaked through the roof and all over the work area.

"Honestly, darling, all that coffee will destroy your stomach," David said. "But if you're determined to venture outside, I'll come along and give you the latest updates."

The rest of the staff passed on coffee, so Meredith and David each donned a maroon Errands, Etc. windbreaker and took the outdoor stairs down to Beans.

The Malibu Town Center was designed to look like an old California mission. It was U-shaped, with a second-floor balcony that wrapped around the building. The design was charming in the normal, temperate Malibu climate, but the wind from the storm seemed to whip itself into a mini tornado and blast up the stairs. Meredith felt a chill through her windbreaker that reminded her of her childhood winters in Montana.

The coffee shop smelled of freshly roasted coffee beans and cinnamon buns. Meredith's usual double espresso and David's usual decaf nonfat vanilla soy latte waited on the counter. Drinks in hand, they settled in a corner booth.

David pulled his smartphone out of his pocket. He typed in something, and the screen brought up a chart. Meredith suppressed a smile. She called David's phone his "fifth appendage," since he was never without it. She had no doubt he could operate the thing with his hands tied behind his back.

David took a sip of his latte and began his afternoon update.

"So we are on track to have Todd and Phil start the outdoor Christmas decorations on Thursday. I told them to pick up a couple of illegals to help out—and don't give me grief about hiring illegals. We pay them cash and the government will never know, and since they don't go into the homes, we don't have to worry about bonding them. Speaking of bonding, I am all over it, darling, so don't you worry. I have Jeanne and Peggy on file, of course, so they will start the indoor decorating on Monday, and we are up to thirty-seven requests for that, so I just hired a cute little Asian girl named Jenny Shu—isn't that an adorable name? I should have her bonded by the end of the week so she can help Jeanne and Peggy, and while I am thinking about it, I have Jeremy gathering the things for the emergency kits; this storm is going to be a doozy. You know how everyone gets when Malibu runs out of electricity, so that's about it. Anything else?"

Meredith took a moment to translate David's run-on delivery. She didn't like hiring illegal day workers, but it was a fact of life in California when you needed a dirty job done quickly and cheaply. To ease her guilt, she insisted the staff feed the illegals a solid meal.

The whole issue of getting new staff bonded was crucial. No one entered a client's home until Meredith had legal proof they were responsible and law-abiding citizens. She kept clients' keys locked in a safe, and she personally handed the keys out to the staff. It was a matter of some irritation to David, but Meredith always wanted to know who was going where and when they returned.

The emergency kits were a new addition to the Errands, Etc. services. The kits contained batteries and a flashlight, matches and aromatherapy candles, a radio, a gallon of Evian water, a French press coffee maker, ground Kona coffee beans, a corkscrew, two bottles of wine, and two cashmere blankets—everything a Malibu resident would need to get through a crisis.

It appeared as if David had the holiday rush well in hand. The storm would slow down the outdoor decorating, but once the weather improved, Todd, Phil, and the illegals could pound out eight houses a day. Meredith felt her stress level ease up. The holiday planning was on schedule despite the weather.

"Sounds like all is under control, David," Meredith said. "Let's send everyone home before the roads close."

David gave a sigh of relief. "Yes, darling. Let's get going."

He no sooner said this than the lights went out. Followed by that odd silence while everyone looked around and wondered where the electricity went. Filled quickly by the gasps of customers waiting in line for their coffees.

"Let's get out of here before there is a riot," Meredith whispered to David.

She wrapped her arms around her waist as they stepped out the door. The rain had started to tank down while they were in Beans, and with it came even gustier winds. Meredith followed David up the stairs, hoping he would block the wind just a bit. She had her head down, her hood covering her face, and didn't see David come to a fast stop. She nearly walked right into him.

David waved at someone on the far end of the balcony.

"Alana! Alana, darling! Do you have your *keys?*"

David raced to the small suite nestled between Errands, Etc. and the offices of their landlord, Lloyd Evans.

David had been thrilled for days when he learned his very best lady friend was to be their new neighbor.

Alana Fox stood at the door to her new office and dangled keys in the air. She smiled and exchanged air kisses with David. Then she turned the keys in the door. David swooped Alana up in his arms and carried her over the threshold. She waved at Meredith as they disappeared inside.

Meredith felt herself shiver, and it had nothing to do with the weather. Alana Fox scared the hell out of her. And that was saying a lot, since Meredith had grown up on a Montana ranch and had stared down danger from a young age. Alana wielded social clout in Malibu like a Montana rattlesnake wields its rattle. And Alana was known to be nasty to women under age forty. At thirty-three Meredith had years to go before Alana Fox would have anything to do with her.

So Meredith had kept her distance but listened with fascination to David's stories. It never ceased to amaze her what busy people would pay to have done for them. She used to think it was ridiculous that her clients paid to have Christmas trees decorated for them. Where was the fun in that? How could someone be too short on time to heat up a batch of hot chocolate, throw some Christmas music on, and argue over where to place the ornaments? And then laugh at how many bare spots were left? But maybe the bare spots were the problem. So many of her clients obsessed over having a perfectly decorated tree with every ornament in the just the right place.

Paying someone to decorate your tree was one thing. But paying someone to find friends for you? Alana Fox charged a fortune to do just that. David called it "establishing a social circle." Meredith thought it was the silliest waste of money she ever had heard of. But then again where would Errands, Etc. be if everyone wanted to take care of the details of their own lives?

She shivered again. And this time it was from the cold. She let herself into Errands, Etc. and went back to managing the lives of people with more money than time.

Chapter Three

"Darling, this is fabulous! We must decorate at once!"

David Currie was beside himself with excitement. We stood just inside the doorway of my brand-new reception area. The lights were out, but I could see there was need for decor. Or at least furniture.

"You need a couple of chairs here in reception and artwork and a receptionist. Maybe Lloyd will loan you one of his blondes, and this door between reception and your office is beyond hideous and…"

And he was off. I let him go and took a moment to let it all sink in. I told myself this new enterprise would be a success. This was a fresh start for me, a new challenge. I found my earlier panic replaced by a promise of possibility, something I had not felt in a long while. The divorce took many things away from me—my husband, my business, my house—and I had spent way too much time being angry about all that. I had forgotten about the rush of energy that comes with a new endeavor. I had missed it.

"So I can start on this first thing tomorrow morning, and by Valentine's Day, it should be mostly done! Won't that be the best gift ever?" David was extremely pleased with his decorating plans, which apparently included knocking down walls and installing a reflecting pool in the reception area.

"How about renting some office furniture and putting a sign on the door?" I countered.

David looked at me as if I had suggested shaving my head and entering a convent. Then he recovered and got serious. Serious David knows how to drive home his point.

"Darling, this office represents you. Your clients are not going to fork over five grand to someone sitting in a rented chair."

"Seven grand. I had to up the price to cover the rent."

David put his hands on my shoulders and stared hard into my eyes. "Fine, darling. Seven grand. All the more reason you must make a good first impression. I can't believe I even had to say this to you, of all people. This space needs paint, quality furniture, original artwork, and a signature scent. I'm thinking tuberose with hints of mint."

I knew better than to argue. Mostly because he was right. The office did need to reflect who I was. Besides the artwork and the signature scent, I would need to throw around a few photos of myself with some A-list Malibu types. Fortunately I had plenty of those.

"OK, David. Paint, decorate, and be done by Friday."

A gust of wind shook the building, and the fluorescent lights in the ceiling flickered. We both looked up. I could tell by David's expression that the fluorescent lights would be the first things to go.

"Darling, if the deadline is Friday, I will have to buy retail."

"Retail it is. Now you need to get home before the roads close."

David knew better than to argue. He lived off Topanga Canyon, just below a favorite mudslide stretch on PCH. I gave him the extra set of keys so he could fill the place with retail. We exchanged hurried good-byes, and off he went.

I took a moment to look around the office again. It felt right. I would make a success of this venture. Sure, the economy was in the tank; homes were worth less than the paper the mortgage was written on; and unemployment was the new black. But regardless of the economy, most folks replace half their friends every seven years. If there was anything I could do, it was help someone find a friend.

For a fee of course.

I shut off the fluorescent lights, locked the door, and headed home myself.

***

Home is a beachfront abode smack-dab on the sand, not far from the Malibu Town Center. Less than a mile actually, so I should have been home in a jiffy.

One of the meanest twists in my divorce was that my ex-husband got the house. The house that I loved with all my heart. So, in all fairness, when he got the house, I made damn sure I got his vintage car collection.

Twelve vintage cars, worth a fortune, I am told. I drive them in a regular rotation to decrease their value. I get a nasty pleasure out of knowing that my ex-husband cringes every time he spots me driving the daylights out of his treasures.

My vehicle that day was a 1956 Plymouth Fury, a pretty white car with gold trim and an ornery reluctance to make right turns. Just as a torrential downpour slammed into town, I negotiated a series of left turns that got me across PCH and past the Malibu Colony Plaza. But then I faced the dead end at Malibu Road. I had to turn right to go home.

It's not that the Fury can't turn right; it's just that it needs a lot of room to do so. I gritted my teeth, hoped like hell no one else expected to use the road, and attempted the turn. I swung left first to make use of every inch in the intersection. Then I swung hard to the right. The Fury complained with a loud creaking sound, the automotive equivalent of nails on a chalkboard. The tires groaned, and the car swung in a graceful wide arc. Up and over the sidewalk, the car headed to the palm tree just outside Spic-and-Span Cleaners. I shoved it into reverse, backed up a few feet, and swung right again. Back over the sidewalk, past the palm tree, and off the sidewalk we went. Then north on Malibu Road, cursing all the way.

Thankfully parking at home required a left turn into the garage. I slammed the Fury's door shut, hit the button to close the garage door, and sprinted down the outside steps to my front door. I got inside as fast as I could and cursed again when I caught sight of myself in the hall mirror.

My clothes were soaked; mascara ran down my face; and you can just imagine what my hair looked like. And I had less than an hour to dress for dinner. Let's just say I was displeased. And I needed to take it out on somebody.

The somebody I chose was Fred.

People with kids have nannies to take care of them. Since I have a collection of cars instead of kids, I have Fred to take care of them. I have room for only one car at a time in my garage, so I keep the extra cars in a warehouse in Calabasas. I keep Fred in an apartment above the warehouse. He tends to their needs and shuttles them back and forth as I need them. I pay the man a small fortune to keep the cars in good running order. He was about to get a piece of my mind.

I found my way to my library at the back of the house, tossed my wet purse on the floor, and dialed Fred.

"Fred here." Fred was home.

"I am sick and tired of that damn car! I cannot go through life turning left all the time! If you don't fix it, I am going to drive it straight to the junkyard!"

There was silence on the other end. I could just see the look on Fred's face. I felt slightly better.

"I am waiting on a part," Fred finally said. "The fifty-six Furies all seemed to stop turning right at the same time, and there's a shortage of gears. I think I've tracked one down in Arizona."

"And this will take how long?"

"A couple of days. Do you want me to bring another car down tonight?"

"Yes," I replied curtly. "Bring the truck."

The truck was a '54 Chevy. And it ran like a dream.

And since I felt better, I added, "Thank you."

And since I didn't want him to think I had gone soft, I hung up.

***

A half hour later, I was showered, remade up, and dressed. And feeling much better.

Then I spotted a toothbrush that wasn't mine.

You must understand that I have lived alone for the better part of seven years. I have to admit, having a place of my own is one of the upsides to divorce. I come and go as I please. I eat what I want, when I want. I listen to the music I like. Things stay where I leave them, and I am a stickler for keeping things out of sight. Call me crazy, but I don't like to see brushes, combs, tweezers, hair dryers, or vibrators lying around on the counter.

But right next to the second sink that I never use, a toothbrush lay on a folded face cloth. It belonged to Stan Sanchez, a cop I had been seeing for a while.

And it bugged the hell out of me.

Don't get me wrong. Stan is everything I like in a man. Tall, dark, intelligent, broad shouldered, he lives out in the Valley, which gives me breathing room. This past morning was one of the rare times we woke up in the same bed. My day started early, so I left him at my home. Apparently he moved in.

I know one toothbrush does not a move-in make. But it is a start. First the grooming items arrive, then a change of underwear, followed by some clothes. Then his food is in my fridge, and before you know it, a gun safe is next to the bed. And that isn't the worst of it. Stan has a shared-custody arrangement with his ex-wife. The objects of the custody are children. If Stan ended up permanently residing in my house, how soon would the children join the grooming items and gun safe?

I told myself I was overreacting. I told myself Stan likely did not want to haul a toothbrush around all day in his patrol car. I thought I could live with the toothbrush in the house if Stan would agree to keep it in the cabinet. I went as far as to think that if the relationship ended, it would be fairly simple to dump the toothbrush in the wastebasket. I talked myself down from the ledge.

By then I really needed a drink.

I tossed my stuff into a dry handbag and made my way downstairs. I braced myself for the possibility that strange items had invaded my kitchen as well. Stuff like beer and salami might be in my fridge. Maybe even something as sinister as white bread had crossed the threshold. Who knew where it would end?

At the bottom of the stairs, my worst fears were realized.

There on the landing lay a duffel bag.

I recognized it as the one Stan had brought along on a weekend getaway we took to Santa Barbara. Sans children. The good news was that it was a small bag, just big enough for a weekend's worth of stuff. The bad news was that it was on the landing at all.

The horror did not end there. From the kitchen wafted the aroma of sautéed garlic and onions. Then the sizzle of chunks of beef tossed into the mix. I recognized this too. Stan's almost famous beef stew.

Stan himself was in the kitchen, all six feet of hunky cop dressed in Levis and a white polo shirt. Making himself right at home, chopping up carrots, an apron around his waist and his gun and holster resting on my breakfast bar. A glass of red wine at the ready, he cooked away in his stocking feet. The man was obviously in for the night.

"I believe I have an intruder," I said. "Should I call the cops?"

"Hey there, gorgeous!" Stan put the knife down and came over to give me a kiss.

Damn him.

My knees didn't actually go weak, but I couldn't have gotten away in a hurry. He smelled of soap as his arms pulled me close. I felt a curious mix of melting into him and a heady spinning. The guy had that effect on me.

Every damn time.

"I tried calling," Stan said, after what seemed like an hour-long kiss. "This storm is expected to make a mess out of the roads, and I have to be on duty early.

I thought I would cook dinner for you in exchange for a bed for the night. That OK?"

He grinned at me with that sexy mouth of his. I felt my irritation at his unannounced arrival fade. But not entirely. I learned the hard way what happens when you let a man get too comfortable in a relationship, and Stan had progressed a little too quickly from leaving a toothbrush lying around to assuming he had the run of my house. Or my bed.

I pulled my cell phone out of my bag. I had turned the volume off before meeting with Lloyd Evans and forgot to turn it back up. Sure enough, there were text messages from Stan. So I had to give him the benefit of the doubt. But not without a small scolding to keep him in line.

"Too bad I missed your call," I said. "I could have saved you the effort of making dinner. I have dinner plans at Grace McDonald's tonight."

"But look! I made 'the Usual.'" Stan opened the fridge and pulled out my favorite drink: gin, limoncello, and diet ginger ale over ice. The gin settles my nerves; the ginger ale settles my stomach without adding calories; and the limoncello prevents scurvy. Pretty much the perfect combination.

Stan set "the Usual" on the breakfast bar with a flourish. And produced another sexy grin. Damn him.

"I appreciate the drink, but Grace is expecting me. I have a rule…"

"I know, you never break a social engagement once you have agreed to attend." Stan turned back to the carrot chopping. "But isn't this a lousy night to have a dinner party?"

"It wasn't lousy weather when we planned it," I said. "Grace has a great new chef cooking tonight. I've been looking forward to this."

So many of my social obligations are just that—obligations. Obligations to dress to the nines and be the perfect guest with all the white lies the role requires. Grace's dinner was an event that I treasured—a gathering of girlfriends who loved good food and wine. We met once a month and hired a chef to cook for us. We talked and ate and drank to our hearts' content. So despite Stan's attempts to woo me with "the Usual" and his yummy stew and killer smile, I was going out.

"You're sure?" Stan looked at me with those big ol' brown eyes of his, and I felt myself waver. Just the teeniest bit.

But the duffel bag on the landing caught my eye, and then I remembered the toothbrush, and then the doorbell rang. It was enough to knock me back to my senses.

"That's my ride. I gotta go." I tossed back "the Usual" and blew him a kiss.

I knew better than to get too close to those brown eyes.

"I'll wait up for you." Stan shot his grin at me.

Again my knees did not go weak. But it took longer than it should have for me to get to the front door.

Damn him.

Chapter Four

On my front doorstep stood a man dressed in a black trench coat and a matching chauffeur's cap. He held an umbrella big enough to keep a small village dry.

"Good evening, Mrs. Fox," he said. He moved the umbrella closer to the door lest a stray raindrop fall on my head.

"Good evening, Jake," I replied. "How are we this evening?"

"We are quite well. Thank you. It has been a good day."

We were not discussing us. Jake's employer is Jorjana York. Jorjana is confined to a wheelchair and is looked after by a slew of devoted servants. Some of her days are good. Some not so much.

Jake delivered me in one dry piece to the limo. I settled in next to Jorjana.

Jorjana York is a beautiful woman in her midfifties. She has shoulder-length curly black hair, a smooth complexion, and dark eyes full of fun. We are not related but she is the one whose name I enter on all those forms requiring a next of kin. She looked particularly gorgeous with her hair piled high on her head and a sparkly set of gold-and-emerald chandelier earrings dancing from her ears.

"Good evening, Alana! What is your opinion of my new carriage?"

Jorjana referred to the limo. She had grown weary of being hauled around town in a bulky white van that strapped her wheelchair to the floor. She said she felt like a cargo delivery every time she arrived anywhere. So the limo had been designed with a special seat that swiveled and allowed Jorjana to be moved easily from the wheelchair directly to the seat. The door on that side of the limo also had been specially designed to be bigger and to swing wider than a regular door. The wheelchair was then stored in a larger-than-normal trunk.

I knew all of this because I had been privy to endless discussions on the creation of the limo. Months of endless discussions. Tonight was the inaugural ride of Jorjana's new wheels.

"It is beautiful," I said. "Comfy too."

"I admit I had my doubts about the interior design. However, I am pleased with the final result. The pink piping suits me, do you not agree?"

Jorjana had been raised all over the world by a diplomat father and a series of proper British nannies. Her manner of speaking is oddly formal until you get used to it.

"I like the piping too," I agreed. The interior of the limo had caused Jorjana angst like you wouldn't believe. She finally settled on leather seats in a color referred to as black, with the pink piping chosen as an accent. I'm telling you, you've never seen such angst.

"I trust your day went well?"

"Great. I signed the lease with Lloyd Evans."

I brought her up to speed on the new office space and David's plans to decorate in retail. We both got a chuckle out of picturing David trying to figure out how to purchase from Pottery Barn. The ability to select an item and have it available immediately would render him speechless. "Speechless" does not come easily to David.

"And Lloyd is well, I assume?" Jorjana said when we stopped laughing.

"Looks great of course. But now that you mention it, he acted funny when I said Francis Ferguson was joining us for dinner—like he was surprised that she was out socializing. Milton's been dead over a year now. It's time for her to get out, don't you think?"

"Perhaps he is concerned that she is venturing out in this inclement weather."

"It seemed more like he was shocked to hear her name. And then he said he hoped she wasn't taking on too much too soon. I thought he and Francis were close friends. It sounded like they hadn't been in touch."

Jorjana considered that for a moment. She got that contemplative look she gets when she is mulling over a problem.

"I do remember some tension between Lloyd and George Ferguson at the memorial for dear Milton. Perhaps Lloyd has kept his distance while the family grieved."

George Ferguson was Milton's son from his first marriage. Tension and George Ferguson are synonymous. The man has the personality of a hung-over baboon.

There was no more time to discuss the matter. The limo pulled into Grace McDonald's driveway precisely on time.

Grace McDonald lives in the hills above Big Rock Beach. Her home is a four-story work of architectural magic. It clings to a steep slope to allow sweeping views of the Pacific. The neighborhood is known as much for its big real-estate prices as for its big views. Not that money is an object of concern for Grace. Her husband makes piles of it doing something no one understands. And Grace makes her own piles selling real estate. Pricey real estate. Grace doesn't bother to get out of bed for a listing under six million. Given the state of the economy, I figured she was sleeping in a lot these days.

"Alana! How are ya?"

Grace met me at the door bearing two glasses of Chardonnay. In lieu of a hug, she handed a glass to me. God, I love this woman.

Grace is a big gal—as in tall, solid, fit. She ran herd on five sons, all with a penchant for running into things so she signed them up to play football. Once the boys were shipped off to college, she dusted off her real-estate license and took up fencing. I suspect she uses the fencing tactics to keep other realtors at bay.

"Where's Jorjana?" Grace asked, as she took my coat.

"Jake is bringing her up now," I said. "Let's stay out of the way while he gets her settled."

Grace led the way into the kitchen. Her house reminds me of those hotels that have soaring atriums from the lobby to the umpteenth floor. The backside of her place is one vast wall of windows, four stories high. Usually the view is spectacular, but the rain poured down the glass like a waterfall.

The main floor is one open area—living, dining, and kitchen. The kitchen is partially separated from the entertainment space by an aquarium just large enough to swim laps in. Tropical fish darted in and out of a coral forest. A puffer fish named Petunia rules the aquarium. Dozing at the base of the aquarium were Grace's golden retrievers, Puppy and Doggy. The fact that I know this just shows how much time I spend at the McDonald place. Grace's home is my refuge of choice when I need an infusion of solid, down-to-earth hospitality. Along with a glass of ice-cold Chardonnay.

In the kitchen a young woman in chef's whites wielded a knife like she meant it. On the stove something earthy and fragrant simmered happily away. A pile of beets complete with leafy green tops lay by the sink. On the counter, a basket of grainy rolls rested in a basket. It looked like the menu would be local, seasonal, organic crap again. I admit I was a little disappointed. I had hoped for something different for a change. Say, fettuccini Alfredo.

"This is Becky Selengut," Grace said. "I met her when she was the guest chef at Rancho La Puerta last spring. Becky can do the most amazing things with sustainable fish. Who knew? Becky, meet Alana Fox."

Becky put down the knife and shook my hand. She was easily as tall as Grace, with short-cropped black hair and eyes that held a hint of mischief. I pegged her at thirty-something, which did nothing to endear her to me. She was thin as well. And you know what they say about skinny chefs.

Becky must have sensed my skepticism. She picked up a tray filled with bite-size appetizers and offered it to me.

"Give this a try. It's braised Sicilian kale on toast with chilies and pine nuts."

My skepticism evaporated with the first bite. Savory spices mixed with salty crunch followed by a gentle kick of heat. I reached for another. Dinner looked more promising.

"We'll just take this out of your way," Grace said, as she grabbed the tray. "Keep it coming, Becky!"

We settled in the living area on oversize couches arranged around a wooden coffee table. Grace's decorating style leans to big and indestructible, likely due to having raised five football players. The upside to her style is that if you spill anything it would be hard to notice.

"I don't think we will have a full table tonight," Grace said. "Last I heard the power is out south of Trancas. Suzanne and Donna may have a tough time getting out of their neighborhood."

"Is your mother still coming?" I asked.

"Yeah, George is bringing her over, and she is going to stay the night. Oh, here's Jorjana!"

Jorjana, wheeled in by Jake, had a smile on her face and not a hair out of place.

Right on Jorjana's wheels came Grace's mother with George.

George Ferguson, he of the nasty temperament, steadied Francis Ferguson with his hands on her shoulders but as far away as his reach would go. He looked, for all the world, like he was taking out smelly garbage.

Francis, however, wore a grin from ear to ear.

The Ferguson family tree is one of those mixed bags of first marriages/children and second marriages/children that is hard to keep straight. George and Grace were half siblings, George being the product of Milton Ferguson's first marriage way back when. Way, way back when. Francis actually raised George, so you would think he would be a little nicer to her. But George is the kind of guy who carries a chip on his shoulder, and you can feel it when he walks into a room.

Grace rose to gather coats and fuss with the seating arrangements.

"Mother, you sit here across from Alana. George, make room for Jorjana."

For a man in his sixties, George was in good shape. Tall, solid, and fit as his sister, he easily slid a massive recliner to one side. Jake wheeled Jorjana into the space and silently took his leave.

"George, can you stay and have drink with us?" Grace asked.

George glared at the glasses of wine on the coffee table.

"Do you have a *real* drink?" He said it as if the lovely Chardonnay were Kool-Aid.

"Yep. Sit down and chat with Alana and Jorjana, and I'll make a martini for you. Oh! There's the phone!" Grace ran off in the direction of the kitchen.

George tossed his raincoat aside and sat on the couch next to me. He glared at me as if I had insulted him. But he glared at Jorjana too, so I didn't take it personally.

"This is such fun," Francis Ferguson said. "Thank you, girls, for including me."

Francis popped a kale-on-toast into her mouth and beamed at us. She looked damn good for eighty plus—a petite woman, with shiny silver hair worn long enough to have movement but short enough to show off a stunning pair of silver hoop earrings. She wore black leggings under a baby-blue cashmere tunic, her feet tucked into ankle boots. It was a flattering, age-appropriate, California-casual look. A classic Malibu style that is a lot harder to pull off than you might think.

"It is our pleasure, Francis," Jorjana replied. "I look forward to our dinner group each month. How long have we gathered, Alana?"

The dinner group grew out of my adjustment to divorce. I love dinner parties, but attending as the lone woman got irritating quickly. Going alone meant I had to be careful whom (which husbands) I talked to. Going with an escort meant an evening of interrogation from bored wives wanting to date vicariously through me. I realized I missed the relaxed companionship of friends.

Girlfriends in particular.

So I solved the problem. I drew up a list of my girlfriends who still ate in public. And who had the means to import a chef to do the work, and the independence to have fun without a guy around. I came up with six names. I proposed we meet every six weeks or so and rotate between our homes. To round out the table to eight, the hostess could invite a guest. Once a year we would hire a car or a plane to take us to the restaurant of the moment. I even came up with a name for the group.

Thus was born The Food Whores.

"We've been getting together for about seven years," I said to Francis, deftly leaving out the official name. "Hard to believe it has been that long."

Grace came back carrying a tray with two glasses of wine, a martini, and a fresh bottle of Chardonnay. What a gal.

"Well, it's just us," she said, as she set down the tray and passed around the drinks. "Camilla called to say she and Mia can't get past a mudslide at Tuna Canyon. And Suzanne just sent a text saying she and Donna were turned around at Decker. We have enough food for an army. George, you want to stay for dinner?"

George took the martini as if he had waited an hour for it to be made. He took a greedy sip but had the decency to give his sister a nod of approval.

"Can't. I have plans."

He settled back on the couch as if expecting a chorus of disappointed groans. None were forthcoming.

"I'm just grateful to be here," Francis said with a nervous glance at George. "I get tired of eating dinner alone."

"Mother, why don't you host a dinner party?" Grace asked. "Becky would love to cook a dinner for you and your friends." Her tone suggested this topic had been discussed before.

"I don't want to be the fifth wheel at a dinner party, even in my own home," Francis said. She too sounded as if this had been discussed before.

"I'm just saying…"

George shot a look at Grace. Grace shut up.

"All your friends are couples, Francis?" I asked, as I felt an idea budding.

"Yes. At least all my friends who are still in Malibu," Francis said. "My widowed friends have all moved to the desert. That's fun when I am there, but most of the time, I am here. And I really hate being the single gal at the table."

"Amen to that," I said. "That is how this group got started."

Becky came around with a platter of scallops drizzled with lemon and perched on top of tiny lentil cakes. My craving for fettuccini Alfredo vanished.

"Sounds like you need a new social group," I told Francis. "Something like an informal dining-out club that meets at local restaurants once a week."

"That sounds *great!*" Grace said.

Francis, however, was not so enthused. "I don't know. Who are these people? What if I don't like them?"

George sighed and rolled his eyes.

Jorjana looked puzzled. But then Jorjana likes everybody.

Despite what you may have heard, I do have empathy. I knew what Francis was afraid of, and it wasn't that she wouldn't like "these people." She came from a generation in which a woman was defined by who she was married to. When Milton passed away, she went from Mrs. Milton Ferguson to Mrs. Francis Ferguson. Her children were grown; her friends had moved away; and her husband was dead. She was alive and healthy and had no idea what she was supposed to do next. Of course she wasn't enthused. She was terrified.

"That's where I can help," I said. "I bet I could find a group of ladies and gentlemen who would love to meet for a meal out. And I can promise you'll like them."

"But I don't like to drive at night…"

"I can arrange for a town car."

"But restaurants can be so noisy…"

"I'll find one that isn't."

"But—"

"Tell you what," I said, before she came up with another excuse and before George's eyes rolled out of his head, "let's meet for lunch tomorrow, and you and I can discuss your concerns. You can be the charter member of the new Malibu Dining Out Club."

She agreed to meet. And not a moment too soon. A blast of wind shook the glass walls of Grace's house, and then the lights went out.

George got up and declared he had to go. No one begged him to stay, not even Francis. Grace produced a flashlight out of nowhere and walked him to the door. There was a muffled exchange between them that did not sound happy. When she returned to the group, Grace poured herself a glass of wine that stopped just short of overflowing.

From the kitchen a glow beckoned. Becky called out that dinner would be served by candlelight, and we'd better eat it before it got cold.

Grace helped her mother up, and I guided Jorjana. The mood of the room relaxed with George's exit. I was glad he didn't stay for dinner and not just because he is a pain in the butt. We enjoy serious girl talk at Food Whores; a man would just hold us back. Plus if George had stayed, I would have felt obligated to invite Stan up. And I didn't want to do that. And, yes, it nagged at me a bit that I didn't want him included in this part of my life.

As we made our way to the table, I gave myself a break and told myself I was onto a good idea. It had been ages since I had come up with a business plan off the top of my head. A social network for seniors was just the project I needed to launch my new office. I could foresee bingo games, square dances, barn raisings— all the things aging folks like to do. I felt a whole new enterprise unfolding.

Little did I know, as I sat to dine by candlelight, that I was in the dark in more ways than one.

Chapter Five

MEREDITH

Meredith Mackenzie awoke Tuesday morning to the sound of a contented purr. It took her a second to remember where she was.

She lay in a heart-shaped bed, her legs tangled in peach silk sheets. The walls of the room were draped in more peach silk, the floors covered by a black fur rug. An antique chaise upholstered in a leopard print sat in a bay window that overlooked the Pacific. Winds whipped at the water, adding frothy peaks to the waves. Seagulls struggled to stay in the air, bouncing around like loose kites.

Meredith got her bearings. She was house-sitting for Chanie Bramlette, a twenty-something celeb of the moment who was out of town filming something stupid but successful.

The source of the purr was Chanie's beloved Persian cat, Baby. The cat slept soundly at the foot of the bed, her purr really more of a snore. Baby was sprawled on her side, legs splayed in every direction, her tail twitching. The cat's sides rose with each inhale and fell with each exhale. Thin strands of long fur took flight on the inhales and were batted into the air by the twitching tail.

Meredith had grown up around cats. But in Montana the cats lived in barns, fed off mice, and generally stayed out of everyone's way. It wasn't until she started house-sitting that Meredith learned she was allergic to them. She felt her nose itch, and she let loose with an "Achoo!" that shook the peach silk bed-curtains.

Baby flew straight up in the air as only a frightened cat can and landed on all fours on the floor. She glared at Meredith with her big blue eyes, and then her contented purr turned into a cough, then into heaving.

Meredith jumped out of bed, scooped up the cat, and raced to the bathroom. She made it to the marble tub just as Baby dislodged a hairball.

"If I had my way, you would sleep in the garage," Meredith said, thinking that a Montana cat would kill for the heated floors in Chanie's garage.

Baby ignored her. She began her morning groom, her back turned to the upchucked hairball. Meredith cleaned up the mess then put out a bowl of organic, fresh cat food from the bedroom fridge stocked with Baby's food and Baby's bottled water. Then she made herself a double espresso from the coffee bar in Chanie's dressing room—a fifteen-by-twenty-five-foot space packed solid with Chanie's collection of size-zero jeans and size-fourteen tank tops.

Meredith lingered for a while in the steam shower while wondering just how long the celeb could keep up this lifestyle. By Meredith's estimate, Chanie's reality series was more than halfway through its run. Meredith gave Chanie less than a year before she ended up in Las Vegas looking for a cheesy stage show willing to put up with her. Maybe Baby could support the two of them by doing cat food commercials.

Meredith made a single espresso while she dressed for work. Her wardrobe consisted of size-eight jeans from the tall-girl section and size-eight tops from the regular women's section. At nearly six feet, Meredith was slim by most standards. By Malibu standards she was practically obese, which explained why she was the house sitter and the Chanie Bramlettes of the world were the stars. Not that it bothered her. In Meredith's book working hard at an honest job beat the hell out of the flash-in-the-pan glitter of Chanie's life. In a year Chanie would be washed up and forgotten, while Meredith would still be sitting at this same house and waking up to the beautiful view of the Pacific. Meredith did hope the next tenant had a decorator with better taste.

She set out a couple of extra bowls of dried food for Baby, tossed her toothbrush, phone and Day-Timer into her tote bag, pulled on a sweater, and said good-bye to the cat. Baby responded with a toss of her head. Meredith secured the house alarm, backed the maroon Errands, Etc. van out of the heated garage, and headed to work.

It didn't take long to see it was going to be a crappy day.

Chanie Bramlette lived on Broad Beach Road, an expensive stretch of beachfront homes between PCH and the ocean. The neighborhood's location on the west side of PCH tended to keep it safe from the regularly scheduled Malibu disasters such as wildfires, floods, and mudslides. But the previous night's storm left even Broad Beach Road a mess. Downed tree branches lay everywhere: on top of cars, in the middle of the road, hanging precariously from power lines. The wind beat at everything left standing. Muddy water streamed down from PCH and across Broad Beach Road like a furious little river. Power appeared to be out at the Trancas Market construction site— and, horribly, at Starbucks. Meredith spotted a line of Malibu moms outside the dark Starbucks, gripping their refillable venti containers for dear life. It was tough enough that the Starbucks had moved to a temporary trailer while a bright and shiny new store was constructed. Now the poor moms were without caffeine as well. Meredith made a mental note to send someone up in a van filled with emergency kits to help the miserable women out.

Just as she turned south on PCH, her cell phone rang.

It was David.

He was in a tizzy.

"Meredith! Darling! Where *are* you? The roof leaked—everything is soaked—and I do mean everything, darling!"

Meredith felt her stomach turn. She forced herself to maintain a voice of reason. Her dad always had said that the true test of a leader is someone who can keep a cool head in a crisis.

"I'm on my way. How bad is it?"

David responded to the calm in her voice. But it did not make things better.

"It is very bad, darling. Very, very bad."

"I'll be there in five minutes."

Traffic on PCH was light, but the road itself was a mess. Little rivers of mud flowed from the rain-soaked hills toward the ocean. Branches lay strewn about, mixed with the odd stray garbage can. Drivers, for once, were polite and took turns at intersections. As far as Meredith could tell, power was out from Trancas Canyon all the way to the Colony, a distance of six miles or so. She made the turn at Cross Creek, passed the Malibu Country Mart, and turned into the Town Center. And slammed on the brakes.

The parking lot in the middle of the Center was flooded. Shop merchants, armed with brooms, frantically swept water away from their doors. In the middle of the parking lot stood a lone truck, up to its hubcaps in water. The truck bed was loaded with sandbags, and the baristas from Beans formed a line from the truck to the shops. The baristas handed sandbags one by one from the truck and stacked them to form a wall against the encroaching water.

Meredith looked up to the second-floor landing. David Currie stood with his phone to his ear, a look of panic on his face. She left the van illegally parked on the street, avoided as much of the flood as possible, and sprinted up the stairs.

"Oh, darling, there you are!" David put his phone in his pocket. "It is awful, just awful!"

Behind David the door to Errands, Etc. was open. Meredith stepped inside, and her tummy gave way to a sickening lurch. It was much worse than a leak. The ceiling in the middle of the room lay open to the sky above. Waterlogged ceiling tiles had fallen onto the worktables in the middle of the room. The gift baskets on the center counter were soaked. The carpet was a soggy mess.

Meredith sloshed her way through the workroom, assessing the damage. The gift baskets were a total loss, but the open shelving sections were dry and the supplies intact. The whiteboard on the wall listing the errands was untouched. The damage seemed to be contained to the center of the room. She walked to the back hallway. The ceilings in her and David's offices were intact. The safe holding all the clients' keys was fine. She gathered the laptops from each office and joined David outside.

David paced back and forth on the landing, running his hands through his hair. He was not alone. A young Asian woman stood uneasily by his side. She looked as if she were ready to jump over the railing and swim through the parking lot to safety.

David took one look at the laptops and paled. Before he could faint, Meredith explained, "Our offices are dry. I just grabbed these to keep them safe. It is not as bad as it looks. The carpet needs replacing, and the gift baskets are a total loss, but mostly we just need the roof fixed."

David's big brown eyes shifted from "deer in the headlights" to "thank goodness, but now what do we do?" He stood in front of her, paralyzed by indecision.

Meredith knew him well enough to give him a problem to solve. "We need to move the worktables and supplies somewhere dry. Any ideas?"

Did he ever. Meredith could practically see the light bulb go off over his head. With a triumphant smile, he pulled a set of keys out of his pocket.

"We can use Alana's new office! It's still empty—we can put a worktable in the reception area and put the whiteboard up on the wall in there and store the supplies in the office, and you and I can work out of our offices, and this is Jenny Shu I told you about yesterday."

Meredith hesitated. The last thing she wanted was to be in debt to Alana Fox.

Another waterlogged tile hit the floor.

Under the circumstances she could think of no other solution.

"Call Alana first and ask her if it's OK," she said to David.

He pulled his cell phone out of his pocket and waved it over his head. "Consider it done, darling!" He spun on his heels and all but sprinted to Alana Fox's new office.

Jenny Shu, the new employee, turned to Meredith in apparent confusion.

Meredith extended her hand in greeting. "Hi, Jenny. I'm Meredith. David hates to admit it, but I am actually the owner of Errands, Etc. Welcome aboard."

Jenny took Meredith's hand and shook it with a surprising strength. She appeared to be in her twenties and of medium height, with close-cropped black hair and a nose ring. She was of Asian American descent, but whether the Asian heritage was Japanese, Korean, or Chinese, Meredith couldn't tell.

"Why don't you go with David?" Meredith said. "I need to check with our landlord about repairing the roof."

Jenny gave her a quick smile and trotted after David.

And Meredith went to deliver the bad news to Lloyd Evans.

***

Lloyd Evans stood in the reception area of his offices, delivering orders to the receptionist, who was also his granddaughter, like an auctioneer spews out bids.

"Angie, get Thompson out here and tell him to bring his best crew. Call Rierdon, and don't let him tell you he can't make it. He's the only plumber I know who has *two* beachfront properties in Malibu. Get the insurance agent on the phone. Wait—I will need to give you his private number. Get every Malibu tenant on the phone, and then forward the call to me. I want to talk to every one of them personally."

Angie took notes on her laptop, her fingernails clicking furiously on the keys.

"And make sure you *write down* all this on paper! If the electricity goes out again, you might not have those notes."

She looked at her grandpa as if he had asked her to carve out notes on stone with a chisel.

"*Paper,* Angie. Don't you have a pen and paper?"

"Do you have a minute, Lloyd?" Meredith never had seen Lloyd so close to frazzled.

On the verge of frazzled or not, Lloyd summoned up a gracious smile. "Of course, Meredith. What can I do for you?"

"Well, there is a hole in our roof..."

She barely had the details out before Lloyd instructed Angie to "Tell Thompson we need *two* crews. And tell him to send the bill directly to the insurance company. Here's that number..."

Meredith felt it best to just leave Lloyd and Angie to finagle the details about a new roof.

The door to Alana Fox's office was open. David and Jenny had been busy in her absence. Peeking inside, Meredith saw a worktable lined up along one wall. Jenny was busily moving in supplies as David hung the whiteboard. It was a cramped solution, but it would work. It would have to. Hopefully Alana Fox would not object to sharing her space.

"There you are, darling!" David stepped away from the whiteboard to admire his handiwork. "What do you think?"

"It's fine for now. What did Alana say about our using her office?"

David's face clouded. "I haven't reached her yet."

Before Meredith had a chance to rake David over the coals, his cell phone rang. A smile spread all over his face as he answered. "Alana, darling! How are you? You won't *believe* what happened last night!"

Chapter Six

Some days start out lousy, and that turns out to be the highlight of the day.

Such was Tuesday.

I didn't wake up so much as I gave up trying to sleep. Storm, surging surf, pounding rain—you name it, it came down long and hard all through the night. Of course the power went out. I stayed in bed and listened to the uproar and Stan's snoring and got just enough shut-eye to be thoroughly cranky at sunrise. By which time Stan had left. With my having no way to make coffee, the only thing that got me out of bed was the need to inspect the storm damage.

I knew it was there. I just knew.

There are a lot of downsides to living in beachfront property. The endlessly annoying sound of the waves, for example. The constant stream of beachcombers past your windows, the seagull droppings on your deck furniture—I could go on and on, and believe me, I do every year when I protest my property taxes. But the worst part of living at the edge of the Pacific Ocean happens with every storm. With the storms come wind and rising tides, and before you know it, the ocean is crashing over your deck railing and knocking at your back door. The only upside to this is the seagull droppings are washed off the deck furniture.

I wrapped myself in my fuzziest robe and found a note from Stan at the top of the stairs.

Hey, gorgeous! Can I stay another night? Roads are a mess, and I might not be able to get back to my place. I'll cook dinner! And I want to hear about your new office. Call me later. —Stan

OK, it was a sweet note. It would have been even sweeter if I could have read it with a cup of steaming-hot coffee. But I couldn't, and I still had to face the storm damage. I made my way downstairs. And lousy turned into rotten.

Just outside my living room's French doors lay the beach. Right where a five-hundred-square-foot deck once stood.

The deck was gone. And so was the furniture with the seagull droppings, the barbecue grill, the bright-red umbrellas, and the nifty all-weather area rug. All gone. In their places were two rickety-looking wooden steps clinging to the house. And then a drop of fifteen feet to the sand.

And me with no possible way of making coffee.

The worst part was that I knew what lay ahead. A call to the insurance company followed by a visit or four from a claims inspector, contacting builders to get estimates, fighting the California Coastal Commission bureaucracy, six weeks of rebuilding, and then repeat it all again in about five years with the next big storm. And for this aggravation, I pay the premium rate in taxes.

I had dealt with this situation enough times to know the best way to proceed was to send a timely e-mail. For an e-mail I needed electricity. With any luck electricity would be available at my swanky new office.

Ten minutes later I was dressed and out the door. I struggled to open the garage door by hand, and rotten turned into crappy. The stupid Fury was still parked inside. Apparently Fred hadn't made it over the hill to switch vehicles. I swore in the most unladylike manner I could summon. I swear that damn car mocked me, laughing at me through its metal grille.

As I backed out of the garage, I dialed David with the last of the battery life in my cell. If there was no electricity at the Town Center, I was going to drive until I found coffee.

David picked up on the first ring.

"Alana, darling! How are you? You won't *believe* what happened last night!"

"You'd better have some great gossip for me. And coffee. *You* won't believe the morning I have had already."

"Coffee awaits, darling. The power just came back on, but now I need the tiniest little favor from you."

"I know about your tiny little favors, David. How much is this going to cost me?"

"Hardly a penny, darling. Now listen, the roof caved in all over the workroom last night, and everything is just a drippy mess, so we moved a few things into your new space just to keep them dry until Lloyd gets a roofer here to fix everything—how far away are you, darling?"

"How many thing are a few things?"

"Not quite all of it. Oh! I see you pulling up—you might want to park on the street unless that tank of yours has water wings."

Then he hung up.

Great. I only had about a million things to do, what with the holidays coming up and all. There were guest lists to infiltrate, hostesses to charm, calls to nearly everyone in town. Not to mention the new project for Francis Ferguson and the other senior citizens in town. For this I needed a solid surface to write on and a door to block out the noise. Something like a private office. Which I thought I had just signed a lease for.

David was right about the parking lot. At first glance it looked like the lot was one big puddle. In the middle was a good-size truck with its wheels halfway submerged in water. The truck held sandbags that were unloaded as fast as you can haul away a fifty-pound bag of wet sand. I left the Fury parked illegally, skirted around the giant puddle, and made it up the stairs just as David's boss walked out of my new office.

Meredith Mackenzie would turn heads in any town but Malibu. She is thirty-three, at least six feet tall, and has legs that go on forever. She has a mop of long dark hair that she wears in a bouncy ponytail, a pretty enough face, and big brown eyes. I knew from David that she had grown up on a ranch in Montana and had a strong work ethic and great business sense. She started Errands, Etc. from nothing and built it into a necessity for most of the households in Malibu. With all that said, I can't say I like her. She is the same age as Little Miss Tight Buns. I have nothing in common with women under age forty and no desire to prove myself wrong.

David swished out just behind Meredith.

"Alana! I have your coffee brewing, darling! Meredith and I have talked it over, and we think you should just use her little office until we sort this all out; she is away most of the day anyway, and you won't need much desk time until the roads open and your clients can get into town…did you hear *all* the roads are closed? We are an *island!* Isn't this too exciting? Now I will just run and get your coffee."

And he disappeared.

Meredith looked as surprised as me that we would share an office. "We could argue with him, but it would be a waste of time, you know." She looked at me with a resigned smile. "I do appreciate the use of your space, Alana, and I will reimburse you for the rent."

It was a nice offer. I was a little surprised someone her age had the graciousness to extend it. The nasty side of me considered accepting. The business side of me knew better.

"Lloyd won't charge us rent under these conditions," I said. "How long will it take to fix your ceiling?"

"I hope not long. The roof repair will be easy enough to do, but the carpet will take time to dry out. Do you want to see if my office will work for you?"

Again I was surprised. I knew damn well that the first she had heard of sharing her office had been when David offered it to me. She operated nicely under pressure, and I really hated to admit to that.

"Let's take a look," I said. "Although, if David is right and we really are an island, I doubt I will have many clients stopping by."

"No kidding," Meredith agreed. "I'm not even sure how many employees I will have today. Everyone lives out in the Valley."

She led the way into Errands, Etc. Even with the knowledge there was a hole in the ceiling, I was not prepared for the mess. The gap was big enough to install an elevator, and it opened clear up to the sky above. The carpet was soaked; water sloshed out when you took a step. The room smelled of rain, wet wool, and disaster. It would be a good long time before Meredith could resume operations. I felt a gaping hole grow in my income.

The back rooms, however, were dry.

Meredith's office was slightly larger than a shoebox. It was painted in a soft shade of gray. A tiny desk faced one wall; an oversize bookcase crowded the other. In lieu of a window, an oil painting of horses running wild hung above the desk. It was an original and very good quality. I couldn't make out the artist's signature, much to my irritation. To add to that irritation, a gun safe prevented the door from opening completely. If I had to guess, I would say that her office was meant to be a walk-in closet.

"This is it," Meredith said. "I am not here much, so David has the larger office. "But you are welcome to use it."

In all honesty I could not see myself meeting new clients in a cramped space accessorized with a gun safe. Even with original art on the wall.

"Thank you, Meredith. It is really nice of you to offer," I said, and I actually meant it. "It will probably be a few days before I am ready to receive clients, so let's see how fast we can get Lloyd to fix everything. Right now I am dying for a cup of coffee."

We sloshed out of Errands. David met us at the threshold of my new office, two cups of coffee in his hands.

"Two coffees! One black, no sugar! One double espresso! Do I know my girls? Why don't you two go back and relax in my office while Jenny and I finish up in here?"

I got the feeling he was trying to keep me out of my new office. This did not sit well with me.

"Why don't I just pop inside and see what the hell you are doing?" I countered as I pushed past him.

My lovely new suite was stocked to the ceiling with all the stuff it took to run Errands, Etc. Wicker baskets, soccer balls, flower vases, cardboard boxes, and toolboxes were stacked in piles on the floor. A portable table was pushed up against one wall; a giant whiteboard hung above it. A little Asian girl stood on the table as she wrote on the whiteboard.

I picked my way through the mess to the back office. There I found ribbons and bows and more baskets. It looked like Santa had dumped his sleigh and beat a path out of town. I can't say I was in the Christmas spirit at that moment.

"Now, darling, I know what you are going to say." David was on my heels.

"No. No, you don't know what I am going to say!" I held up my hand to stop him. Because I am a mature woman, I took a deep breath—that and the fact that Meredith had handled the turn of events so well. Damn her.

"I understand why you needed to move out of your space," I said. "And I even get why you thought moving in here would work. What I don't understand is why you thought it was OK to do this without asking me first. What the hell were you thinking?"

I had every right to be upset.

I probably didn't need to yell at him.

David's mouth dropped open. His big brown eyes widened. He seemed to shrink right in front of me. I don't think I ever had yelled at him before. But then he never had taken anything of mine before.

I do not take kindly to others helping themselves to my stuff. From the day my cousin swiped my Easy-Bake Oven to the day Little Miss Tight Buns swiped my husband, I have been notoriously selfish about sharing. Honestly, I would have said yes to letting Errands, Etc. move into my office. But David should have asked first.

Still I didn't have to yell.

Just then Lloyd Evans walked in. "Alana, David, I do understand your concerns."

Lloyd's voice held empathy and calm. Which just pissed me off even more.

"I have a roofing crew on the way."

Of course he did. No one could get in or out of Malibu, but Lloyd Evans had a roofing crew ready to go.

"David, there is another problem," Lloyd continued. "It seems the power outage has played havoc with my computer system. Do you have anyone on staff who can straighten it out?"

David looked immensely relieved at having an excuse to ignore me. "Our tech guru can't get in," he said. "Let me call around and see who—"

"I can do it," the little Asian girl said. "I used to work in tech support at Fresno State."

"I don't know, Jenny," David said. "We don't have your bonding papers yet and—"

"My computers are frozen," Lloyd told her. "Can you fix that?"

"Sure. That's a common problem after a power failure," Jenny said. "It might take an hour or two, though."

"I need Jenny here to—"

"Don't be silly, David," Lloyd said. "No one is going to need Errands today. Jenny, is it? Come with me."

Lloyd took Jenny by the arm, and that was that.

And David was left to face me.

"Alana," he began.

My turn to interrupt.

"David, I shouldn't have yelled at you. But you should have asked first."

"I know, darling. How can I make it up to you?"

I knew just how. I pulled my insurance card out of my bag and handed it to him.

"Call my insurance agent and tell him my deck is gone again. He can send the claims inspector out anytime. I am taking Francis Ferguson out to lunch today, but I will be home by two. Thanks!"

I left him there to sit on call, waiting all day. Served him right.

Chapter Seven

I had arranged to meet Francis Ferguson for lunch at Wasabi, an Asian-style bistro close enough to the water to see your sushi swimming around before you eat it. The building has housed an Italian pasta palace, a Mexican taco joint, a Spanish tapas bar, and a steakhouse in all the years I have lived in Malibu. My favorite, to date, is Wasabi. The sushi is fresh, the sake piping hot, and the seating arranged so every diner gets a nice tufted leather booth with an ocean view. It is a good spot to settle in and have a long, leisurely conversation. Which was just what I intended to do with Francis.

I was full of great ideas thanks to a night of practically no sleep. I had a plan to start a seniors' social club. The only sticking point being that I didn't know too many old folks. With any luck, however, Francis Ferguson did. All her friends couldn't be dead already. All I needed to get started was two of her friends, because building a social circle is really just a matter of numbers. If two of Francis's friends each had two friends, I'd have six new contacts. With that as my starting point, I'd know everyone in town over age eighty inside of three weeks.

Traffic was light on PCH. It looked like most Malibu residents were staying home. Or maybe it just was that everyone figured the whole universe was without electricity. Fortunately the block that held Wasabi had lights. A neon sign glowed at the front door declaring the place O EN.

I pulled up to the valet with enough time to give the kid intricate instructions on how to drive the Fury. He opted to leave the thing right out front. Can't say I blamed him.

I was seated in my favorite booth, had some sake on order, and was preparing to silence my phone when the stupid thing rang.

It was Stan.

It took me until the third ring to answer. It always does. Whenever I see his photo pop up on the screen, something in my gut leaps. It's not butterflies, and it's not nausea; it's a disturbing cross between the two, and it leaves me a little short of breath. Damn him.

"Hey, there," I said with as much nonchalance as I could manage.

"Hey, gorgeous! It is a mess out here. All the roads in and out of town are closed. Are we on for dinner?" Stan sounded weary.

Stan is a Malibu/Lost Hills cop. The territory they patrol is a convoluted mix of beachfront mansions, rural ranches, wilderness canyons, and everything in between. It is hard enough on sunny days to keep an eye on it all. Toss in lousy weather, floods, and mudslides, and it was no wonder Stan sounded tuckered out.

Ironically Stan made a job change from homicide to patrol cop in hopes of having a more predictable work schedule. He took this path of career suicide because he wanted to be available for his kids. Didn't look like that would happen this week.

Fortunately I knew just how to cheer the guy up.

"Dinner sounds great," I said, as I wondered whether my black satin unmentionables were clean. "Did you notice my back deck was gone?"

"No! Oh, man, Alana, I'm sorry. I was out of the house before dawn. I'll take a look at it tonight. Where are you?"

"At Wasabi for lunch. No worries about the deck. David is getting hold of my insurance agent. I've done this before."

I had done this before. Twice before actually. But this was the first time I had a guy in my life willing to "take a look" at the mess. I kind of liked it. Almost enough to forgive the toothbrush. Not enough to feel guilty about leaving him alone for dinner while I dined with girlfriends. But enough to wear something naughty to bed.

"When do you get off duty?" I asked.

I felt badly for him. He really did sound exhausted. We spent a few minutes figuring out who would be where and ended up agreeing to meet later at my new office so he could see it. Before I could tell him about the roof missing at Errands, Etc., he was called away. To what I had no idea.

Presently Francis arrived with Grace in tow. Francis wore the chic outfit of tunic and leggings from the night before. Grace wore an expression of worry and determination.

"Sorry to be late delivering Mom," Grace said, as I rose to give her a hug. "It is a little treacherous getting down the hill today."

The three of us exchanged quick pleasantries and mumbled concerns about the weather.

"Mom insists on going back to her house after lunch," Grace said, and she didn't look happy about it.

"I will be just fine in my own home," Francis said.

I got the feeling yet another topic had been thoroughly discussed.

"That house is solid adobe, and George just changed all the batteries in my flashlights. Now stop arguing, and let us enjoy our lunch. The sooner we get done, the sooner you can pick me up and take me home. It's not getting any nicer outside."

We all looked out the window. If anything it was getting uglier. On the horizon loomed a line of black clouds that looked as nasty as any I have ever seen. The ocean was so black, it looked like asphalt. I gave us a half an hour before the next storm hit.

"I'll take Francis home," I told Grace. "It's not that far from my place. You'd better get back up the hill while you still can."

Grace hesitated for a nanosecond. "All right. Thank you, Alana. I'll have the valet toss Mother's bag in your car. But you will make sure everything is OK and call me?"

"I will call. Now go."

And she was off.

"This is just swell." Francis smiled as she looked around. "I love the decor. The last time Milton and I were here, it was a Mexican restaurant."

"It seems to change often; that's for sure. What do you feel like eating?"

Francis had a very adventurous palate. She ordered unagi, spicy tuna roll, something with oysters, and the daily special, which I swore sounded liked "brine of roe soaked in halibut sweat." I decided on the scallop roll and miso soup and another round of sake. Francis preferred the sweet plum wine.

"Cheers!" I said when the drinks arrived.

"*Kanpai!*" Francis returned.

"Been to Japan?" I asked, impressed.

"Often," she said. "Milton produced martial arts movies in Japan. I went along whenever I could. It's a swell country. So clean and orderly."

"Did you travel with him often?"

"Boy, did I!" Francis brightened just at the thought. "We had wonderful luck with housekeepers, so I was able to leave the kids and run around with Milton whenever he was on location. We spent a lot of time in Spain and Italy in the fifties and sixties. And then there was that boom in Japanese films in the eighties. I had a ball!"

"Sounds like fun," I agreed. "You must miss Milton."

Her smile dimmed a bit at that. "I do miss him. I miss him terribly. But Milton would have wanted me to enjoy the rest of my life. I'm sure he would."

"Well, I have some great ideas for you then," I said.

The food arrived, and I laid out my plans for a seniors' social club. It sounded better out loud than it had in my head. I was pretty proud of myself.

Francis, however, seemed underwhelmed.

"What's the matter?" I asked. "This isn't what you had in mind?"

She tossed back the last of her plum wine and signaled the waiter to bring another. My kind of gal.

"Your plans sound swell, Alana, but there is something I would like you to help me with first."

She dug into her purse and brought out a well-worn leather journal. The journal was hand tooled with a design of vines and the initials "FM" intertwined. Francis pulled out a black-and-white photo and gave it to me.

The shot was of four young women on the beach in San Diego with the Hotel del Coronado in the background. Judging from the silly skirted swimsuits the girls wore, the photo was from the 1940s. I recognized one of the girls as Francis.

"I came to Los Angeles when I was eighteen," she explained. "I was a very good seamstress, so I landed a job in the wardrobe department at one of the movie studios. These three gals and I all worked at the studio, and we became fast friends. We saved our money up and took the train down to San Diego for a weekend whenever we could."

She took the photo back from me. "This is Dot Derringer. Next to her is Pat Scott, then me. Then Celeste Monte. We used to have such a swell time. We used to dream about what it would be like to stay at the hotel and drink Tom Collinses on the verandas."

Francis's eyes misted up. She looked at the photo the way you look at your high-school yearbook, with bittersweet memories.

"When was this photo taken?" I asked.

"I guess around nineteen forty-five," Francis said. Her misty eyes hardened the tiniest bit. Something about the memory was not all sandy beaches and Tom Collinses.

"We grew apart when I fell in love with Milton," Francis said. "He was everything to me. I don't regret that for a minute, mind you, but now that he's gone, well, things are different. I do want to build a new social life, but first I want to mend a few fences from my old life. I feel bad about letting these friendships drop. I would like to reconnect with these girls and take them all to the Hotel Del. To fulfill an old dream, I guess. Can you help me, Alana?"

"That's not what I usually do." I hesitated because something told me she wasn't telling me everything. "Can't you get Grace to help you with this?"

"I want to keep my children out of this. They know me as Francis Ferguson and feel my life started when I married their father," she said. "These girls were a part of my life when I was Frannie Martin."

"You said you grew apart. It sounds to me like something bad happened. What are you not telling me?" I had no intention of taking on a new role without knowing what I was getting into.

That took her by surprise. I braced myself for a convoluted dissertation on how she wasn't lying and the fact that I didn't understand and how I could say such a thing. She surprised me by just coming clean.

"I'm afraid they won't see me," she admitted.

"Why?"

"It's a long story."

"Then you'd better get started. We don't have a lot of time before that storm hits."

It took another glass of plum wine, but she got it out.

"I met Pat Scott when I first got to LA. We both roomed at the same boardinghouse. She helped me get that job as a seamstress. We met Dot and Celeste on the lot. They were both working as dancers or actresses or what have you. I really liked those gals because they were full of fun. We all wanted to better ourselves and see the world. That's how we started going to San Diego. Whenever we could scrape the money together and get the time off, we hopped on the train and off we went. San Diego wasn't as nice then as it is now, but we found a cheap boardinghouse on Coronado and spent the days on the beach. We had big ideas about meeting the handsome officers staying at the Hotel del Coronado."

Francis paused long enough to finish her plum wine.

"We were young. And foolish enough to think marrying would solve all our problems. Anyway, we had fun. Of course our lives all changed eventually. Pat was the first to move away. She inherited some money and decided to go to nursing school. Dot married a magician and went on the road with him. Celeste and I were left to fend for ourselves, and that ended badly."

"How so?" I have to admit, I was intrigued.

"Well, Celeste was dating Milton before me. Suffice it to say that when he left her and started seeing me, our friendship was over."

She saw the look on my face.

"I know, Alana, I shouldn't have taken up with him, but oh, he was so charismatic! I justified it by telling myself that Celeste was juggling a lot of men at once, and she wouldn't miss losing one of them. She was a gorgeous girl, and the men just hung off her. I didn't realize until too late that she was crazy about Milton."

"Why didn't you just end things with him?" I asked.

"It was too late by then. We were madly in love."

"So you and Milton got married. How did Celeste react to that?"

"Well, we didn't get married right away." Francis blushed. "I'm not proud of this but, when we fell in love, Milton was still married to his first wife, and she was pregnant."

You could have knocked me over with a marshmallow about then. Milton Ferguson, the blowhard I remembered as a paragon of right-wing family values, had fooled around on his pregnant wife with not one but two sweet young things?

"So Milton got a divorce and then you married?"

It occurred to me that the conversation had taken a sharp turn away from organizing a quiet little seniors' social club.

"No. The baby was stillborn. And Lydia—that was Milton's first wife—was devastated. So Milton adopted George. But then Lydia got tuberculosis and died."

As I look back on it, my first mistake was in not focusing on the surprise that George was adopted. I should have asked why she said, "Milton adopted George" instead of "Milton and Lydia adopted George." But I was still reeling from the image of Milton Ferguson as a three-timing cheater. My curiosity followed the sordid tale of adultery times three.

"And then you got married."

"Yes, a year later. And to answer your question, Celeste had married a lovely man by then and moved on with her life. I was devoted to Milton and our life together. I let everyone from my life as Frannie Martin go. Now I regret that."

"I gotta say, that is quite a story. But I still don't see why you need me to do this. Why don't you send them an e-mail and see what they say?"

Francis shook her head. "No, I want to look each one in her eyes and apologize for my behavior. But I'm afraid they won't see me. If you pave the way for me, it would help."

"What do you mean by 'pave the way'?"

Francis reached back in her purse and pulled out three envelopes. Ivory paper, heavy gauge. The kind of quality stationery that everyone in Francis's generation always has on hand. I would have bet a mint that the paper was embossed with the letterhead "Mrs. Milton Ferguson."

Each envelope was addressed in very good penmanship and written in fountain pen.

"I've written letters to each one. If you would hand deliver them and explain what I have in mind, it would be swell. I have their addresses here."

She handed the envelopes to me along with the addresses for each woman. All lived in Southern California. Pat Scott lived in Malibu.

"Please, Alana, it would mean so much to me."

What could I say? Her story was fascinating. And what the heck, if things worked out, Francis and her three girlfriends could form the core of my new seniors' social club. Starting with three friends just put me that much further ahead.

But I was off my game and unfortunately didn't realize it. I was stunned over the revelations I'd heard and wrongly focused on starting a new venture. It never occurred to me to ask Francis how she acquired the addresses and married names of friends she hadn't had contact with in sixty years.

That was my second mistake.

Chapter Eight

The Ferguson solid-adobe house lay in an obscure corner of Corral Canyon about as far in as you could go. Fortunately most of it was paved. Unfortunately there were a hell of a lot of right turns. By the time I pulled the Fury onto the Ferguson property, I had worked up quite a sweat.

"Milton hated Plymouths," Francis said. "He was a Cadillac man."

"I hate Plymouths too." I thought of my reliable Chevy truck. "Give me a Chevy any day."

But as much as I cursed the damn steering, the Fury kept us warm and dry. The second storm slammed into Malibu just as we left Wasabi. Torrential rain pounded the windshield and poured across the PCH. The wind was strong enough to have blown a lesser car clear into San Fernando Valley. Although it was midafternoon, it was dark enough to need headlights. The AM radio worked well enough to let us know that all Malibu roads were closed. No one was getting in or out of town unless the storm conjured up a tornado and blew them out of there.

I had been to parties at Francis's before, so I knew the Ferguson spread took up four wooded acres and consisted of the solid-adobe house, a small barn, an equestrian arena, and the requisite pool and tennis court. For all the money Milton had sunk into the place, you would have thought he could have sprung for paving the drive. Sadly the approach to the house was one hundred yards of packed gravel, most of which had washed away by the time Francis and I drove up. I gunned the Fury and prayed we could get to the front door on sheer will.

We almost did. The Fury did its level best and powered its way to just short of the circular driveway. Then it stopped with a sickening whirl of the wheels spinning without traction.

"That sounds bad, Alana," Francis said.

"I think we're stuck," I replied. "Let's make a run for the house. I'll need to call a tow truck."

I knew as soon as the words were out of my mouth that the odds of getting a tow truck all the way to the back of Corral Canyon were nil. Thank God Francis had a nice guest room. It looked like I'd be there for the night.

"Let's go through the garage," she said, pulling a remote opener out of her bag. I had to wonder just what else she kept in there. Journals, photos of old friends, garage door openers. With any luck she had a number for a trusty tow truck. Truth was, I really wanted to go home if at all possible. I felt myself needing Stan Sanchez's attention, regardless of how tired the man was.

Francis aimed the remote at the garage, and the door slid open. I took a deep breath, as if I were about to swim to the garage. We hurried up the driveway and arrived to the garage at the same time. Just as the lights went out.

"Oh, great," I moaned.

"It's OK, Alana," Francis said. "This door opens to the mud room, and that's where I keep the flashlights."

I rethought my expectations and envisioned sipping a lovely Cabernet by a roaring fire. Milton had a legendary wine cellar. I could change my wet clothes and don the fuzzy guest robes I just knew Francis had, build a fire in the fireplace, open one of Milton's exquisite wines, and wait out the storm—as soon as I called Stan and changed all the plans I had for him. Damn it.

Francis opened the door to the mud room. The house was still and as dark as the middle of the night. I heard her open a drawer and rummage around.

"Oh, here it is!"

I heard a click, and a flashlight lit in Francis's hand. A look of triumph crossed her face. She was standing at a bank of cabinets. Just beyond the span of the flashlight, I spotted a hallway leading to the main house. Francis smiled and turned to light the way. I stepped over the threshold, and the door shut behind me. Francis turned to look at me, and her smile turned to shock.

"What?" I heard her cry out.

Then something hard whacked the back of my head. It sounded like a gun going off inside my skull.

I felt a sudden nauseating dizziness, and my legs folded beneath me. I tried to catch myself on one of the cabinets, but my right shoulder took the brunt of my fall. Searing pain raced through my right arm. And that's all I remember.

Chapter Nine

MEREDITH

Meredith Mackenzie tried like hell to get a grip. The roofers Lloyd Evans had so efficiently produced had to stop repairs because the next storm blew in so fast that all they could do was nail down plastic tarps. The tarps had lasted all of ten minutes before being blown to God knew where. Rain again poured through the open roof. The water soaked the carpet to the point that it leaked through to the coffee shop below.

Meredith locked the door to Errands with a sigh. Not only was her business a sodden mess, but the baristas at Beans likely would never comp her espresso again. It had been a seriously rotten day.

To make things worse—because, really, they weren't bad enough—Lloyd Evans's office had sprung leaks. Lloyd's granddaughter and his other blonde assistants broke their nails setting out buckets to catch the drips. So Lloyd too moved his operations into Alana's suite. His computer sat on top of a stack of plastic storage bins in the back room. Jenny Shu worked furiously all day to retrieve the data that Lloyd's computers had misplaced during the power outages.

Normal activities in Malibu were put on hold as everyone struggled to survive the storms. No soccer practices, no dry cleaning to pick up, no gift baskets to deliver, no holiday decorations to brighten anyone's day. It was all "hunker on down and pray to survive." Meredith convinced Jenny, Lloyd, and the blondes to leave early with the mantra of the day: "Get home while you still can."

Meredith thought ever so briefly about Chanie Bramlette's Persian cat. Poor thing was all alone. Meredith had lied through her teeth to Chanie earlier in the day and swore Baby wasn't traumatized by the weather. Even so, she knew Baby would be fine. She'd left three days' worth of food and water for the stupid cat. Meanwhile Meredith had to figure out how to run her business out of a veritable closet—while the cat slept on eight-hundred-count sheets.

When Meredith walked into the veritable closet, David Currie was busy working the phones. Or phone. He did have just the one, but he played it like it was an entire symphony orchestra. He talked as he made furious notes on the whiteboard.

"Yes, Suzanna, darling, we are here, but we can't get to you. Kanan Dume Road is closed! We have you on the board, and we will come to you as soon as we can. Hello, Terry. Are you *frantic*? Do you have power? Oh, too bad, darling, just open a bottle of Chardonnay before it warms up. Hello, Jeanne? Darling, how *are* you?"

And on and on. David touched bases with as many clients as he could reach, listened to their complaints, and then booked errands into the New Year. The man was worth twice what Meredith paid him, and she paid him a king's ransom as it was.

She was just about to tell him to go home for the night when the door to Alana's/Errands, Etc.'s/Lloyd's office opened. In walked Stan Sanchez.

Stan stopped just inside the door with a look of confusion. His left hand moved in the direction of his gun, the cop in him alerted that something was amiss. His hair was wet, and he smelled of shampoo and soap. He was freshly shaven but looked as if he hadn't slept in a week.

Meredith had to hand it to Alana. Of all the available men in Malibu, Stan Sanchez had to be the hunkiest. Of course the guy was old enough to be, well, Meredith's uncle, but he was gorgeous. He was tall—always a plus in Meredith's book—fit, calm, and focused. He looked like the kind of guy who could take down a bank robber at noon then show up to grill the hot dogs at the family barbecue. Meredith liked that in a man—strength and softness. And it didn't hurt that he wore his Levis like a second skin.

Stan's eyes landed on Meredith, and his gun hand relaxed.

"Hey, Meredith!" Stan said. "What's going on here? Where's Alana?"

"We had a leak in our roof, so we moved in here," Meredith answered.

"Does Alana know?"

Stan's voice was guarded. She found it interesting that even this big burly cop was wary of crossing Alana.

"Yes, she knows," Meredith said.

"I'm supposed to meet her here." Stan looked at a loss as to what to do next. Which Meredith found adorable.

"Have a seat." Meredith pulled out a folding chair. "She's probably stuck in traffic somewhere."

"Grace, *darling!* Whatever can I do for you?" David said. He waved at Stan and held up one finger, indicating he would be done quickly.

"Why, no, I don't know where Alana is, but Stan is here and he..." David raised his eyebrows in Stan's direction.

Stan shook his head.

"No, darling, Stan hasn't heard from her either... really? Lunch? And she never called? That doesn't sound like her, no. Well, I will ask Meredith, and we will get back to you. I'm sure everything is fine...what with the power outages and all. Yes, I will get back to you. Bye!"

David put his phone down on the folding table.

"That was Grace McDonald. She delivered her mother to have lunch with Alana at Wasabi at noon. Alana was going to take Francis home. Grace hasn't heard from either of them. And they aren't answering their phones."

Stan pulled his cell from his pocket and dialed.

Meredith pulled her cell from her pocket, located Francis Ferguson's home number from the Errands Etc client list and dialed.

Neither of them got an answer.

"Where does this woman live?" Stan barked.

"Oh, darlings, what do you think happened?" David wailed, as he retrieved the address from his trusty phone.

Stan's phone made a god-awful beeping sound.

"Sanchez here." He listened for a moment then hung up. "I have to go. Can you guys check on Alana and this other woman? They aren't at Alana's place. I just came from there. Keep me posted!" And he was out the door.

"Darling, I have the address right here," David said to Meredith. "It's up Corral Canyon."

"Let's go!" Meredith grabbed her maroon Errands, Etc. windbreaker and her tote bag. "We'll take the truck."

David hesitated. "Darling, it is a mess out there. Maybe we should call for help?"

"David, a Malibu cop just told us to go find her ourselves. If there was help available, don't you think Stan would have called for it?"

"Oh, yes, well, maybe. I'll just give Alana another little buzz to be sure."

He talked to himself. Meredith was already out the door.

***

The maroon Errands, Etc. truck was a Ford Super Duty model with a V-8 engine and the kind of traction control rarely needed on paved roads. Normally the truck stood out in Malibu traffic as the only American made vehicle in town. As Meredith and David drove north on PCH, the truck stood out as the *only* vehicle on the road.

"Have you been to Francis's house?" Meredith asked.

Francis Ferguson rarely used Errands services and Meredith was not in the same social circle as the Ferguson/McDonald clans, so she never had visited the Ferguson place.

"Oh, yes, darling! It is just fabulous! Such a pretty setting and—"

"How far up the canyon is it?" Meredith interrupted.

She had a hard time seeing where she was driving. It was just sunset but as dark as night. Power appeared to be out all along PCH, eliminating any ambient light from homes. The rain pelted down so hard, the windshield wipers could not keep up. Corral Canyon Road rose high into the hills before descending back down into the canyon. Meredith could only imagine how muddy the road on the canyon floor would be.

"Actually you take the low road just before Corral Canyon," David said with dread in his voice. "The Ferguson place is on a private road at the bottom of the canyon."

"Great."

Meredith gritted her teeth and followed David's directions, turning east onto a paved road. If it was dark along PCH, Corral Canyon was an abyss. The truck's headlights illuminated only enough for her to see muddy water streaming from the hillsides across the road. They drove slowly as the road wound its way. Meredith knew the road led to small ranchettes of horse property. There were no lights on in any of the homes along the way. After an eternity, David pointed to the right, and Meredith turned the truck onto a gravel road.

Or what was left of a gravel road. The road quickly turned into a muddy path strewn with fallen branches. Meredith was never more grateful for having the extra traction. Even then the truck struggled through the sludge, slipping sideways at one point and bouncing off a fence. Meredith managed to right the truck by turning into the slide, using the advice her father had given her for driving in the Montana snow.

"There's Alana's car!" David cried out.

Alana's Plymouth Fury sat at an odd angle to the side of the gravel drive. Meredith thought it was a strange place to leave a car in the middle of a rainstorm. Why didn't she park closer to the house?

Then the truck's headlights shone on the Fury's tires. The tires were mired in the muck, halfway up the rims. Meredith could tell from the pile of mud at the rear of the car that Alana had tried to power her way out, but she only had succeeded in burying the car deeper in the mess.

"Let's leave the truck here," Meredith said. "It looks like the mud is worse closer to the house."

"I am so glad we found them!" David exclaimed. "I will just call Grace right now." He started dialing.

But something was wrong. Meredith could just feel it.

"You have cell service here? Then why haven't they called?"

David stopped in mid dial. "I don't...well...oh, darling...they are OK, aren't they?"

Meredith didn't answer. She turned off the engine and reached into her tote bag. She pulled out a gun.

"Stick close to me, David. And keep that phone on."

Chapter Ten

I came to and heard myself moan—deep, primal moans that demanded the attention of all my being. I lay on my back. It was dark. It was hard to breathe. How long had I been here? Each exhale came out as a moan. Each inhale brought searing pain.

My right shoulder was injured; there was no doubt. It lay at my side in an odd angle, as if partly detached from my body. My head ached worse than any hangover ever. I tried to roll over. My right shoulder seemed to stay behind then sent out shots of pain, forcing me back on the floor.

I lay there long enough to gather my wits. Something told me to take a physical inventory of my injuries. My feet, legs, and hips seemed OK. My left shoulder and arm were fine. My right arm was numb; I couldn't move it. The right shoulder was definitely in the wrong place. My neck was wrenched. The headache threatened to bust right out of my skull. But I was alive.

Where was Francis?

Then I remembered what had put me on the floor. I had followed Francis into the house. She had cried out. Something whacked me on the back of the head. And then what?

I contained my moaning long enough to listen. I heard the wind outside and rain pounding on the roof. The house itself was still. Too still.

I braced my right shoulder with my left hand and used my abs to get myself to a seated position. My head spun, and I felt the sushi from lunch do a somersault in my stomach. I willed myself not to throw up. Or pass out. I scooted myself around so my back was against the cabinets and pushed myself up with my legs.

It was really, really dark. The kind of thick dark that is hard to move around in even when you know where you are. All I knew for certain was that I was in Francis's mud room. I remembered she said her flashlights were stored in a drawer. I opened the first drawer I could feel. As my left hand let go of my right shoulder, it felt like a loose pendulum swinging from my torso. And it hurt like nothing had ever hurt in my life.

I propped my right arm up on the counter and fumbled through drawers until I found a small flashlight. I listened again before switching it on. I heard only wind and rain. No sound of another person anywhere nearby. I didn't know whether to be relieved or terrified.

I switched on the flashlight and put it in my mouth. I couldn't move without stabilizing my right arm with my left hand. Ahead of me lay the kitchen. I went that way, hoping to find a phone.

The Ferguson kitchen was a generous space laid out around a center island big enough to land a plane on. Lots of solid-oak cabinetry, granite, and stainless steel. The drawers lay open, and kitchen stuff was flung about.

I saw every appliance known to mankind, including a pizza oven. But no phone.

Swinging doors led to the dining area. I stood at the doors and listened again. Still just wind and rain. I slid through the doors and passed through the dining room to the living room.

The living room stretched from the front of the house to the back. A giant fireplace dominated the room. Pillows were strewn about. A sofa was upturned. The drawers from the cocktail table were turned upside down and emptied of their contents.

A short reception hall led to the front door, which lay wide open. The wind blew the rain over the threshold, drenching the tile floor.

I didn't know whether the open door meant the attacker had left or was just outside hailing a cab. I stood stock-still, afraid to even breathe. The only noise was the wind and rain. The only light was the narrow stream beaming from the flashlight in my mouth.

Beyond the living room, a hallway led in two directions. I hoped to find Francis hiding under the bed in the master bedroom. I turned to the back of the house, remembering the master bedroom faced the backyard. The hallway was wide and carpeted. On the walls hung photos of the Ferguson clan through-out the years. Double doors at the end of the hallway lay wide open.

I found the master bedroom in a mess. Drawers were pulled out and turned upside down. The linens were stripped from the bed, and the mattress was upended and leaning against a wall. Pictures were scattered on the floor. A hallway led to the bathroom. Along the way I passed two walk-in closets. Clothes lay on the floor, shoes tossed about. His and hers closets with his and hers clothes. Francis hadn't yet parted with Milton's things.

I found Francis on the floor in the bathroom. She lay crumpled by the bathtub. She was on her back, her arms askew, her eyes closed. There looked to be a long scratch down the side of her cheek, barely enough to break the skin.

I knelt by her side. I bolstered my right arm on my knee and reached for her wrist.

There was no pulse. A shiver ran through me.

She was dead.

I swung the flashlight around the bathroom. Were there no telephones in the Ferguson house? The light landed on a door that opened to a small room with the toilet. Sure enough, a phone hung on the wall in there of all places. I picked up the phone. The line was dead.

My head spun. I took the flashlight out of my mouth and leaned against a wall. I felt hot and cold and nauseous. I felt like I could use a long nap, and I had just enough wits about me to realize I had a concussion. I closed my eyes with a thump.

A thump?

I opened my eyes and heard the thump again. Or was it footsteps?

It *was* footsteps. And hushed voices.

90

Voices?

There were two of them?

I frantically swung the flashlight around, looking for something, anything that I could use to defend myself.

Next to the toilet was a plunger—a heavy-duty one fortunately. It had a rubber bottom but a hefty metal rod. I switched off the flashlight, tucked my right hand into my waistband to stabilize my shoulder, picked up the plunger, and held my breath.

The footsteps made it into the bedroom. They were headed my way. I inched my way out of the loo to hide behind the bathroom door. My plan was to jump out of the dark, whack them with the plunger, and run for it. It was a lousy idea, but it was all I had.

I stood with my back to the wall and waited for them to enter the bathroom. I raised the plunger over my head. Two people came through the door. I stepped behind them and yelled, "*Hey!*" as I swung the plunger at their heads.

They both jumped out of the way, and I missed them entirely.

In a nanosecond I recognized David.

Then Meredith Mackenzie knocked me out with a wicked left hook.

Chapter Eleven

"Alana, darling! Alana! Oh, sweetie, are you OK?"
David Currie said, as he knelt at my side. "She's awake!
Everyone, she's awake!"

As I opened my eyes, I saw David hovering over me
and a uniformed cop standing guarding over Francis. I
heard Meredith Mackenzie's voice from the bedroom.
Bright streams of light from flashlights swirled about,
doing nothing for my headache.

"Darling, the police are here," David said. "Stan is on
his way. Don't get up."

My jaw felt as bad as my shoulder.

"Did Meredith punch me?" I asked David.

"Well, yes, darling, but you did jump out of nowhere.
You're lucky she didn't shoot you."

"Shoot me? She had a gun?"

"She is from Montana, darling."

I heard more voices in the bedroom. One of them
was Stan's. I was so relieved to hear his voice, I sat right
up. Big mistake. My head spun; nausea overwhelmed
me. My lunch vaulted right out of my stomach and all
over my lap. David took a step back, looking a little ill
himself. I felt wretched. I almost wished Meredith had
shot me and put an end to my misery.

And then Stan was at my side. He produced a cool, wet washcloth out of nowhere and wiped my face. He cleaned up my lap. He fashioned a sling for my arm out of a clean white shirt that likely had belonged to Milton. He did all of this while issuing firm directions to everyone around

"We can't get you to a hospital, Alana," Stan said. "All the roads are closed. And power is out at the urgent-care center, so we can't send you there either. There's a doctor nearby, though, so Meredith and David will take you there, OK?"

"OK. Francis is dead. My shoulder hurts. And Meredith punched me."

I was babbling, and I knew it, but I couldn't stop myself.

Stan stroked my head and made reassuring noises. He and David helped me to my feet. My knees were wobbly; I wasn't at all sure my legs would support my body. Stan grabbed my left arm to keep me upright and reached around my back to steady my right arm. David walked behind us, his hands holding tight to my waist. Meredith followed, no gun in sight. One cop stayed with Francis. I was glad she wasn't alone.

We made it through the house and through the rain to Meredith's truck, one of those macho machines with four doors and room for bales of hay. Stan and David settled me in the backseat. Meredith fetched pillows. I was belted in. Stan gave me a kiss right on my sushi-vomit lips. And to think I was annoyed with his leaving his toothbrush on my counter.

"I gotta stay until Homicide gets here," Stan said. "Can you tell me what happened?"

I could. I thought I did a pretty good job of it, but for some reason, Stan looked worried.

He turned to David and Meredith. "Can you guys give me a second here with my lady?"

I thought that was the sweetest thing ever and fully expected another kiss.

"Listen to everything I am about to tell you, Alana."

Stan looked me right in the eyes with his serious cop face on.

Or two cop faces—I was starting to see double.

"The Homicide guys are going to want to talk to you. Do *not* talk to them unless you have a lawyer present. Do you understand?"

"Well, yes, but why?"

"You're going to be their first suspect."

"What?"

"Just trust me on this. The first thing they're going to think is that you injured yourself attacking Mrs. Ferguson."

"Why would I attack her? This doesn't make any—"

"Yeah, I know…this looks to me like you two interrupted a robbery. But when someone is dead, Homicide's process is to eliminate suspects. You're just the first in line. Remember, I used to do that job. So promise me you'll get a lawyer."

"OK. I guess."

"Good. We never had this conversation, OK?"

"OK."

Stan waved David and Meredith back over.

"Take good care of her," Stan said. "The doctor's expecting you."

David and Meredith piled into the truck, and off we went. The drive through the canyon was dark, bumpy, and painful. Meredith handled the truck well; I'll give her that. She kept it mostly on the road and mumbled "Sorry" every time we hit a pothole. I couldn't respond; it was all I could do to keep my arm immobile and not think about Francis.

It wasn't until we reached PCH that I realized I had no idea where we were going. A doctor could be anywhere. Doctors, lawyers, and actors make up most of the population in Malibu—an interdependent set of relationships if there ever was one.

"Where does the doctor live?" I asked.

Silence from the front seat. I did not take this as a good sign.

"We are not going to the doctor's home, darling," David finally said. "We are going to where the doctor is…uh…staying."

With that Meredith turned the truck into the drive that led to Sosei.

Malibu is known for a variety of wonders—among them the sun, the beaches, the mountains, and the ridiculous real-estate prices. In recent years rehab became big business in Malibu. Clinics have popped up like California poppies in the spring, and they are lucrative enough that a new place seems to open every time a mega mansion goes into foreclosure. What else are you going to do with a seventeen-bedroom, twenty-bath structure with three pools and four tennis courts?

Sosei was named after the Japanese word for resurrection. The proprietors purchased a sprawling foreclosed estate on ten acres, put in a koi pond, and redid the interior of the place to look like a Japanese teahouse. And they made it so exclusive that there isn't even a sign on the gate.

Sosei is my idea of hell. It specializes in all-day meditation classes, a vegan menu, and no alcohol. It's enough to drive you to drink.

"You aren't going to leave me here are you?" I cried out.

"Shh, darling. It will be fine."

"Do not leave me here. I mean it, David!"

Meredith and David exchanged a look, which did nothing to reassure me. My head was splitting; my arm felt like Meredith really had shot me; and a lovely woman was dead. If ever there was a time I needed a drink, this was it.

Meredith pulled up to a wooden gate and rolled down her window.

"Yes?" a voice spoke through an intercom.

"We have Alana Fox to see the doctor," Meredith said.

"Come in."

The gate rolled to one side, and we were in.

"Am I going to see the staff doctor?" I asked, while hoping Sosei at least had pain-killers on hand.

"No, darling. You are going to see one of the patients who just happens to be a doctor as well."

"You're taking me to see a doctor committed to a rehab clinic?"

"Well, yes, darling. There are no other doctors available right now. Stan said it is OK. The paramedics have taken people to him all night. He even delivered a baby!"

One of the few downsides to living in Malibu is there is no hospital. With all the roads closed and power out at the urgent-care center, I understood I had to take what I could get. I just hoped the baby was delivered and sent home. The last thing I wanted to do was to listen a screaming brat.

Well, actually, the last thing I wanted was to be admitted to an alcoholic rehab center.

The entrance to Sosei was covered by a thatched roof and blocked by an ambulance. Meredith parked behind the ambulance, and she and David did a decent job of extracting me from the backseat of the truck. They all but carried me through the front door. Waiting just inside was an efficient-looking woman dressed in a Japanese farmer's coat and loose cotton pants. Apparently the Japanese theme extended to the staff uniforms. Just like Disneyland.

"Mrs. Fox? Please come this way. Dr. Moss is waiting for you."

I got a vague impression of lots of rustic wood and bamboo decor. Honestly Hello Kitty and a Shinto priest could have greeted us at the front door for all I cared. My headache had reached epic proportions, and I was having trouble focusing. I did note a lot of people lying around the lobby on cots, which I suspected was not the usual routine. To my relief, no one was nursing a newborn.

Meredith and David got me into a room with an examining table and set me on top of it. The efficient woman told them to wait outside and closed the door.

"I'm Katherine, and I will be assisting Dr. Moss tonight," she said. "Tell me what happened."

I did. She took notes on a pad of paper. Then she produced a blood-pressure cuff and a thermometer and proceeded to take my vital signs. She asked the usual questions about medications. She wrote everything down, and then the doctor arrived.

He was a handsome guy, forty-ish and in good enough shape. He was dressed casually in khakis and a polo shirt. I would have found it hard to believe he was in rehab if not for the crazy shaking of his hands. It looked like he was trying to shake them dry.

"I'm Dr. Moss," he said. "We will do what we can for you."

"We" was his entourage. There was a security guard the size of an NFL linebacker. Next to him was an EMT dressed in scrubs. Next to him was a lawyer; he was the only guy wearing a tie and smelling of lawsuits.

"Before we begin, Mrs. Fox, we must go over a few details."

This came from the lawyer, who produced a stack of papers. The long and short of it was that I understood that Dr. Moss and Sosei were in no way, shape, or form responsible for anything that happened to me—or my dependents for the next twelve generations. I signed with my left hand and wondered how the mother of the newborn baby had felt at that point.

Dr. Moss proceeded with his examination. He asked me what happened. He asked whether I was allergic to any medications. He took my pulse. He shone a light into my eyes. He gently took the improvised sling off my arm, and then the nurse cut my sleeve away. He pinched my fingers and asked if it hurt. It didn't. I really couldn't feel much at all. He prodded at my jaw and asked me to open and close my mouth. He whispered something to the EMT, and the guy scurried away. The security guard and the lawyer stayed put.

"You have a concussion, Mrs. Fox," Dr. Moss said. "For that I prescribe rest and avoiding alcohol. Your jaw is badly bruised, so you should apply ice packs every twenty minutes. We have an x-ray machine here, so Katherine will take you there so we can see what is going on with your shoulder. I will see you back here in a few minutes."

With that he left. As he walked out of the room, his entire body twitched to one side, and he fell into the doorjamb. The linebacker steadied him with a gigantic paw and followed him down the hall. If I had felt at all well, I would have worried about the medical care I was receiving.

Katherine helped me down from the exam table. She showed me how to steady my arm. She covered me with one of those awful robes that open in the back. She settled me in a wheelchair. And off we went to x-ray.

I will say this about Sosei, if they served drinks, you would never need to leave the place. Just outside the x-ray room, a sign indicated that the saunas, steam rooms, pools, tennis courts, shops, and restaurants were over by the Sosei Spa. It was just one margarita away from a world-class resort.

Thankfully the x-ray process went quickly. I vaguely remember moving from the wheelchair to a cold table and a technician aiming something at my shoulder. Katherine had me back into the exam room and up on the table before my head spun off my neck. By that time I was too dizzy to notice whether Dr. Moss made it back into the room without taking out the doorjamb.

The EMT came back carrying an IV bag.

The security guard/linebacker stood in front of me and put his hands on my legs.

Katherine tucked my left arm under hers.

Under normal circumstances, I would have suspected something. But I had been whacked on the head, injured my shoulder, discovered my friend dead, and been socked in the jaw. So I wasn't exactly on my game.

"Your shoulder isn't broken, Mrs. Fox," Dr. Moss said, as he held up the film to the light. "It is dislocated, so we will need to pop it back into its socket," he added, as if he were arranging a meeting for coffee. "We're going to start an IV on you that includes some pain-killers."

Apparently that paper I signed had a provision for not asking questions. Before I knew it, a needle went up my left arm, and the EMT held the IV bag over my head. The linebacker bore down on my legs. Dr. Moss placed his hands in front of and behind my right shoulder and pushed like he was slamming a door shut. The most excruciating pain I've ever experienced shot from my shoulder, through my arm, and flew out my fingertips.

It hurt too much to scream. It hurt too much to breathe. It didn't hurt too much to vomit. The sad remains of my lunch hurled out of my stomach and splattered all over Dr. Moss's khaki pants. Served the guy right.

I will say this, as soon as I vomited, my shoulder felt immediately better. Sore as hell but much, much better.

Whatever was in the IV was my new favorite beverage. It was as if I had downed four margaritas without the brain freeze.

My shoulder was back in its intended place, which pleased me to no end. I went on and on about how much better I felt and how glad I was that I had met them, and gee, we should all get together more often. About the time I asked to kiss the new baby, David and Meredith were summoned.

I vaguely remember pouring back into Meredith's truck, doctor's orders in hand. I had a bright new shiny sling for my shoulder, an ice pack for my jaw, a lovely new Japanese farmer's coat and a prescription for a pain-killer. David informed me that Jorjana was expecting me, and yes, he did agree that a summer barbecue was a good idea. And that was the last thing I remember about Tuesday.

Chapter Twelve

MEREDITH

Meredith Mackenzie shifted the truck into gear and pulled away from Sosei, never so happy to get the hell out of one place in her life.

Sosei represented every self-indulgent obsession she could not understand. The hot-rock massages, the mind-numbing soothing music, the endless cups of hot tea. And hours and hours of focus on how Christmas in the third grade just ruined your life. Meredith believed everyone was about as sober as they made their minds up to be. And yeah, the world wasn't fair. So get over it. Try a little self-discipline for a change and just don't pick up that first drink.

In the backseat David Currie sat next to Alana Fox, doing his damnedest to keep her upright.

Meredith never had seen Alana in such a mess. Her hair stuck out at all angles; mascara ran down her face; and she smelled of vomit. Alana's right arm was supported in a sling, and she wore a Japanese farmer's coat over what was left of her Ralph Lauren cotton shirt.

She babbled on and on—some nonsense about hosting a barbecue at Sosei just as soon as the weather improved. She illustrated her barbecue plans with her left arm and kept whacking David in the head.

"Darling, you must be still," David said to Alana as he tried to pin her arm down. "The doctor said you must rest and be quiet. Quiet, darling. *Quiet!*"

"I'll be quiet. I promish. I'll..." Then her head fell forward, and she was out.

"*Oh*, thank God!" David's relief was palpable. He gently settled Alana's head on his shoulder. "Meredith, darling, how fast can you make it to Jorjana's?"

"In no time at all. We have the road to ourselves."

PCH was deserted. Not that the going was easy. Sheets and sheets of relentless rain pelted the road. Water, mud, and debris swept over the pavement like a shallow river. Power appeared to be out everywhere. The headlights on the truck were barely able to illuminate enough for Meredith to see where she was driving. From the gate at Sosei to the bottom of the hill that led to the York Estate, a distance of three miles, Meredith did not pass a single vehicle.

David, meanwhile, had his phone in hand and was on the line to Jorjana. "Alana will be fine, darling. No you can't talk to her. She is just...um...a little bit asleep right now. We'll be there in a jiffy."

David had worked the phone like a bloodhound on a scent, hunting down an orthopedic surgeon at UCLA; updating Stan and Jorjana on Alana's condition; getting the loopy Dr. Moss to call in a prescription for pain medications; then arranging a conference call between the orthopedist, Dr. Moss, and Jorjana's nursing staff and demanding everyone come up with a plan for Alana's recovery right then and there. Meredith wasn't surprised by David's organization, which was per usual for him. She was surprised by his fierce determination to obtain the very best care for his friend amid the storm, power outages, mudslides, and all. Meredith thought it touching—and found herself just a little bit envious.

"Jorjana's staff is waiting for us, darling," David said. "It turns out they have all the pain meds on hand if Alana needs them."

The gate leading to the Estate was open. Meredith drove up the steep, winding drive to the palatial structure that Jorjana York called home. Built on a bluff that overlooked downtown Malibu, the York Estate was composed of a house slightly smaller than a shopping mall, sixteen manicured acres of grounds, two swimming pools, two tennis courts, and a separate garage for a fleet of cars. The live-in staff had their own housing complex at the back of the grounds. Of course the entire estate appeared to have power.

The York night staff stood at attention at the front door. A nurse dressed in scrubs held on to a gurney; two maids dressed in black with white aprons held blankets; and the house manager dressed in suit and tie held on to Jorjana's wheelchair. Jorjana was wrapped up in a quilted robe and wore a look of contained panic on her face.

Meredith parked under the cover of the porte cochere. The nurse and the maids helped David dislodge Alana from the truck. Alana was out cold, so it was like trying to unload a side of beef. The nurse tucked blankets around her, and the maids pushed the gurney up the ramp and into the house. Jorjana watched the whole operation, clasping and unclasping her hands, her eyes filled with worry.

The house manager turned her wheelchair to move her inside. Jorjana stopped him with a raised hand. "Please, do come in, Meredith," Jorjana said. "You must eat."

Meredith almost declined the invite. Then she thought of the long drive back to Broad Beach Road and Chanie Bramlette's stupid cat and the poor provisions in Chanie's fridge. It was all she could do to keep from vaulting over Jorjana and into the warm, lighted, peopled house.

The foyer of Jorjana's house was big enough to hold an ice rink. Double stairs led to the second floor. The ceiling was a domed contraption that Meredith knew could be opened to the sky. The floor was marble. The furniture was ancient. Turn to the right, and you wandered into a reception hall that overlooked the pool and led to a dining room that comfortably sat a hundred. Turn to the left, and you wandered through another reception hall that overlooked the other half of the pool and led to the west wing of the house. Meredith followed the house manager and Jorjana through carved mahogany doors to the left.

Of the two reception areas, Meredith preferred this one. The smaller of the two, it was paneled in dark wood. Thick Oriental rugs covered the floor, and the furniture divided the room into intimate seating areas. Meredith's favorite feature was the fireplace. It was big enough to walk into. She was happy to find a wood fire burning furiously, filling the room with the scent of cedar. Every light was on. It felt cozy, bright, and safe.

The house manager settled Jorjana near the fire at a table set for three. Sandwiches, fruit, and cookies were stacked on a tiered platter. Iced water was poured into stemmed goblets. The plates were fine bone china and the serving pieces solid silver. A tray held a china teapot and three cups and saucers. The house manager set the brake on Jorjana's wheelchair and silently disappeared.

Somewhere in the room, a clock chimed nine times. Nine o'clock. No wonder Meredith was starving.

"May I offer you some tea?" Jorjana asked. "Unless you prefer something stronger."

"Tea is perfect. Thank you." Meredith took a seat close to the fire and reevaluated her earlier criticism of the beverage.

"Please serve yourself," Jorjana said as she poured the tea. "David will join us presently."

A small menu lay next to the tiered platter. The sandwich selection was limited to rare roast beef on rye with grainy mustard, tomato, and marinated onion; turkey on sourdough with cranberry and orange compote; Jarlsberg cheese on grainy wheat with avocado, sprouts, and tomato. If none of those met your pleasure, the chef gladly would grill up anything.

Meredith was too hungry to wait for a grilled anything. She took one roast beef and one turkey sandwich, added some sliced mango from the fruits, and dug in. Two bites in, she felt herself relax. Four bites finished off the roast beef. Her turkey sandwich was nearly gone when David reappeared.

"Alana is *sound* asleep. Nurse Terry is a *doll*," David whispered, as if Alana were asleep in the next room. He flopped down on the chair opposite Meredith and shook open a linen napkin. With a sigh he stared at the feast laid out on the table.

"Is that *tea?* Oh, Jorjana, I need a real drink!"

Jorjana picked up a small crystal bell near the teapot. From somewhere a maid appeared with a drink on a silver platter. How the maid knew what to bring was beyond Meredith. David took the drink, downed it in one gulp, and asked for another.

"David, please do tell me. What happened? I cannot believe Francis is gone." Jorjana cradled her teacup close to her face.

David's face was the curious color of gray that follows a shock. Meredith knew it only too well. She distracted herself by reaching for another sandwich as David filled Jorjana in. With one hand holding Jorjana's and the other clasping his drink, David spoke in a hushed voice.

"Alana took Francis to lunch today. It seems Francis was ready to socialize again, and Alana, of course, is the perfect one to help with all that. The weather, as you know, was just awful, but Francis insisted…"

Meredith tuned out just then. Hearing it all over again was more than she could handle at the moment. She already had gathered from Stan that Alana and Francis had surprised a burglar. A safe had been opened in one of the closets, and whatever was in there had been rifled. Meredith took a macadamia nut cookie from the top tier and waited for David to finish. As he went on, his voice rose as his freshly filled drink disappeared. It was efficiently replaced with a third drink. By the end of that drink, he was delivering the story with his usual overstatement.

"…and then—*pow!*—Meredith socked her right in the jaw!"

"She jumped out of nowhere! She scared the crap out of me!" Meredith objected then added, "Sorry, Jorjana."

Jorjana took Meredith's hand and gently squeezed. Jorjana's hand was ice cold.

"The authorities believe a burglar is to blame?" Jorjana asked.

"Yes, darling. Stan said it has all the hallmarks of a breaking and entering. By the way, Stan told me to make sure Alana gets an attorney."

"Whatever for?"

"Really?"

Both Meredith and Jorjana were surprised.

"Stan said the Homicide detectives will talk to her as soon as she is awake, and the first thing they will do is eliminate her as a suspect, and we aren't supposed to tell the detectives Stan said so." David took four cookies from the platter. "I left a message at Richard's house and told him to get here first thing in the morning."

"Richard? As in Richard Lafferty?" Meredith asked. "You have Richard Lafferty's home number?" She knew she shouldn't be surprised that David could contact Malibu's most famous criminal-defense attorney at home. But still she was. And more than a little impressed.

"I have *all* of Richard's numbers, but now that you mention it, I probably should leave a message with his girl as well. Excuse me."

While David placed his call, Meredith finished her tea. She was well fed, warm, safe, and suddenly exhausted. And not at all interested in driving back to Chanie Bramlette's place.

Apparently Jorjana read her mind.

"Meredith, you must stay the night. The weather is much too inclement to hazard a drive home."

"Thank you, Jorjana. I really am tired. I'm not even sure which roads are still open." The stupid cat would live until morning.

Jorjana picked up another little bell, this one brass, and gave it a tinkle. Out of nowhere, again a maid appeared.

"Ms. Mackenzie is staying the night, Andee," Jorjana said. "Please prepare the blue room in the west wing for her. Mr. Currie will stay as well. Please prepare the green room for him."

"Of course, Mrs. York," Andee replied, and disappeared.

"OK, that is all taken care of." David walked back in. "I spoke to Richard's girl. She will make sure he is here at nine. Jorjana, do you mind if I stay?"

"Andee is just preparing your room and a room for Meredith in the west wing," Jorjana replied. "I am afraid that I must retire now. David, will you see that Meredith has everything she needs?"

Jorjana picked up a bell again, this one silver. Yet another maid surfaced. A round of good nights and the maid took Jorjana away. Meredith stifled a yawn just as the clock chimed eleven.

"I'm beat, David. I left my stuff in the truck. Do you suppose Jorjana has an extra toothbrush around here?"

"No worries, darling. Everything you could possibly need will be in the room. You'll die when you see the west wing."

Meredith winced at his choice of words.

Chapter Thirteen

I awoke Wednesday morning in a four-poster bed made with fine cotton sheets, a fluffy comforter, and down pillows. The room was decorated in soft blues and ivory. The curtains were open, and it appeared the rain had stopped. A wood fire burned in a fireplace. On the mantel were framed photos of Jorjana and me in various spots around the world. I knew I was in my suite at the York Estate. What I couldn't understand was why a nurse and a lawyer were arguing in the doorway.

The lawyer was Richard Lafferty, a criminal-defense guy. Richard is a big man who spent his undergrad years majoring in sacking quarterbacks and minoring in mayhem. He was good enough at both to get into law school, where he learned to refine his bullying techniques to fit a courtroom setting. If you are in trouble with the law, Richard Lafferty is the guy you want on your side.

The nurse was one of Jorjana's loyal caregivers. Nurse Terry was half Richard's size physically but his equal in the stubbornness category. She glared up at him as she barricaded the doorway with both arms.

"She needs her sleep!" Terry whispered.

"I don't have time to wait for her to wake up!" Richard whispered back.

"Whisper" is a relative description. They were both loud enough for me to hear across the room.

"I'm awake," I said from the depths of the down and cotton. "What are you doing here, Richard?"

"Mrs. Fox..." Nurse Terry began.

"Alana, what have you done..." Richard Lafferty began.

"What the...*ow!*" I made the mistake of trying to sit up. Every cell in my body ached, starting from my head, which pounded like a jackhammer; through my shoulder, which felt like a knife sliced through it; down to my toes, which just hurt for the hell of it. I smelled like vomit. Yet another day was not getting off to a good start.

"Mr. Lafferty, please give me a moment to help Mrs. Fox get up," Terry pleaded as she raced to my side.

Richard took a better look at me and stopped in his tracks. Apparently I was a sight.

"Ten minutes," he grumbled, and out the door he went.

Terry applied that magic that nurses have and managed to get me out of bed and into the bathroom. She got me into a hot shower, helped me soap and shampoo everything that needed it, and dried me off. Then she gave me something for pain and searched the closet for clothes. I keep personal items in my suite, such as clothes, shoes, toiletries, makeup, a checkbook, cold Chardonnay, and jammies. There have been times when

I've kept myself there as well. Like just after my divorce or when recovering from the flu.

Terry found an easy outfit to get me into, supported my arm in the sling, and had me upright in a chair with a cup of coffee inside of an hour.

Richard, of course, hadn't waited. Terry handed a phone to me.

"Mr. Lafferty told me to have you call as soon as possible," she said. Then, because she's one of Jorjana's well-trained staff members, she stepped out of the room.

"What the hell have you done now?" Richard barked from his cell phone.

"I've done nothing," I replied in all truthfulness for once. "I got knocked out and dislocated my shoulder, and I have a concussion. How do you know about this? What were you doing here?"

"David left messages for me all over hell and back. Jorjana wrote a check once again to retain me as your attorney. I know Francis Ferguson is dead, and you were with her. Tell me what happened. So help me God, Alana, tell me the truth."

Stan's warning about being a suspect came back to me loud and clear. Truth be told, I was a little peeved about being suspected when I was innocent. For once.

But I was in pain and shaken up enough to want protection. So I told Richard what I remembered.

"And that's all of it?" Richard demanded when I finished.

"Yes."

"You aren't leaving anything out?"

"No."

Silence on Richard's end. Then a sigh.

"If you are telling me the truth, Alana, we should be OK. But do *not* talk to the cops without my being present. Do you understand?"

"Yes, but—"

"No buts! Call me the second you hear from them. Tell them to meet you at my home. I'm turning around right now, and I'll work from the house today. Do *not* talk to them without me. Do you hear me, Alana?"

"Yes."

"And what are you going to do when you hear from them?"

Normally if someone talks to me like I am six years old, I tend to ignore what they are saying and do whatever I damn well please. But Richard Lafferty and I have a history together. This was not the first time he was retained to get me out of a jam. I have learned that ignoring his advice tends to make matters worse and judges cranky. So I disregarded his tone and opted to do what he said.

"I will tell them to meet me at your house," I said.

"Good." He proceeded to have me recite his address, his phone numbers, his fax number, and the number to a local cab service.

"No excuses, Alana." Then he hung up.

My reply was unladylike at best.

Nurse Terry reappeared with a smile and an offer I couldn't refuse.

"Mrs. York would like you to join her for breakfast." Sounded like the best idea anyone had all day.

***

Breakfast was served in Jorjana's bedroom suite just a mile or so down the hall from mine. Perhaps it was the effect of the pain-killers, but I found walking with my right arm strapped to me difficult at best. With the help of Nurse Terry's steady arm, I didn't stumble and take out a priceless Ming vase along the way.

I was glad to have a companion with me for another reason. Between my suite and Jorjana's, there were any number of nooks and crannies where a stranger could jump out and whack me over the head. I kept Nurse Terry close by my side in case I needed to use her as a shield against attack.

We found Jorjana in her morning room, a fire in the fireplace, a breakfast table set for four, and David Currie at her side. David jumped up and helped Nurse Terry settle me in a comfy chair. She then took her leave.

Jorjana's suite is decorated to suit her taste. The walls are painted lavender, the furniture upholstered in ivory satins; the artwork favors floral landscapes. Recorded music from a harp played in the background; the musician was Jorjana herself.

Unless you were looking for it, you'd never notice how the suite is also designed to accommodate Jorjana's needs. Distances between furniture groupings look appropriate instead of pushed aside to make way for a wheelchair. The carpet feels sleek, not thin. Wider doorways are arched and graceful. Medical call buttons are discreetly placed. In the bedroom Jorjana's specially made bed is swathed in miles of lavender silk.

David and Jorjana were conversing in hushed tones when I entered the room. Neither of them looked like they had enjoyed a good night's sleep. Jorjana was dressed for her day in jeans and a cowl-neck sweater. Her eyes had dark circles under them. David looked like he had picked his clothes out of a pile from the laundry-room floor. His eyes were red and puffy.

"Did you sleep well? Are you in pain?" Jorjana asked me.

"I'm sore, and my head aches. I'm not sure how well I slept. I've had enough pain-killers to put down a moose."

That seemed to satisfy her. She visibly relaxed, settling back with a cup of coffee.

"Meredith left at the crack of dawn," David said, as he pointed to the fourth place setting. "Are you at all hungry?"

I was famished.

A platter of muffins and pastries sat in the middle of the table alongside a large bowl of fresh fruit. A maid appeared out of nowhere and set down a cup of black coffee. The sound of the coffee cup landing on the linen tablecloth scared the crap out of me. My left arm shot out from my side and whacked the maid right in the stomach. She let out a soft cry and then, as any well-trained York employee does, apologized.

Jorjana frowned.

David raised an eyebrow.

I felt like an idiot.

Unperturbed, the maid placed a blueberry muffin on my plate, cut it into bite-sized pieces, and disappeared, hand to her stomach. I picked up a fork in my left hand with all the grace of a toddler wielding chopsticks. I took a stab at the muffin, and it slid off the fork and landed in my lap. I picked it up as discreetly as possible and put it back on the plate. I tried again. This time the muffin made it halfway to my mouth before falling off the fork, bouncing off my chest, and landing on the floor in a crumble.

"Why don't you just use your fingers, darling?" David suggested.

"Yes, please do. We need not stand on formalities, under the circumstances," Jorjana added.

I picked up a piece of muffin and tried to put it in my mouth. Easier said than done. My jaw was so sore that I could barely get my mouth open. With a sigh I settled for coffee.

"Meredith had the presence of mind to retrieve your bag from your car last night," Jorjana said. "David, please hand Alana's bag to her. I am certain she will need the use of her cellular phone."

David grabbed my bag from a nearby chair. He peered inside then pulled out my phone.

"You do have messages, darling." He turned the phone to me. "See? One from me, one from Stan, me again...I was *frantic* at that point, darling...Stan again, me again, Stan again…oh! Here's a strange number! Shall we have a listen?"

David put the phone on speaker, and we all listened to Detective Somebody or Other telling me to return his call. Not ask, mind you. He told me. I wasn't feeling up to my usual self enough to ignore the command and wait for him call me again. I asked David to dial the number, and before you could say, "You have the right to remain silent," I had an appointment with the detective within the hour at Richard Lafferty's house. As far as I could tell, the detective wasn't at all surprised at my request to have an attorney present.

I had to wonder whether that didn't make me look the tiniest bit guilty.

I've often thought that Jorjana and David could organize the whole world if they put their minds to it. Such was the case after I finished my call with the detective. Jorjana summoned her hair and makeup gal to put me into some semblance of "pulled together." David raced through his phone to rearrange his morning so he could go with me to Richard's house. Jorjana instructed her social secretary to tend to my calls and the meetings that were on my calendar and to reschedule into the next week. David called Fred and broke the news about the Fury getting stuck in the mud. Then he looked up the latest road closures and announced we could get to Richard's place without using the York Hummer. The Bentley would be just fine. The activity in Jorjana's morning room reached a pitch equal to the situation room of any government.

I surprised myself by letting them take over. Once the gal had pulled my hair and face together, I managed to wrestle my phone away from the social secretary. All on my own, I found a calm corner in the room. Once my head stopped spinning from the effort, I watched the craziness put forth on my behalf and counted my blessings for a change.

Jorjana and David are my family now. My parents divorced when I was eight, and I put an end to the weekend visits with my father when I was ten. My mother died of a broken heart drowned in cheap wine when I was in my thirties. I have no siblings. Along the way I learned that biological families aren't what they're cracked up to be, and it's better to just build your own family. The guy I married wanted to do that by having kids. After we divorced and he went on to spawn offspring with Little Miss Tight Buns, I gathered my closest friends closer.

Interestingly enough, both Jorjana and David had their own reasons to build a custom family. Jorjana lost her only child in a skiing accident, the same accident that put her in the wheelchair. Her husband, Franklin, is devoted to her but soothes his grief over the loss of their little girl by leaving for long periods to go shoot wild things all over the world. David was the oldest child in a family that lost their mother when he was twelve. He ran the household and lorded over his brother and sister until they were out of high school. When he gathered the courage to tell his father that he was gay, the ungrateful bastard threw him out of the house. David has not spoken to his father since.

So the three of us bonded over family tragedies and loss. And I have to say, the relationships have been the best two of my life.

Then, like a nudge to remind me, my phone rang. It was Stan.

His face came on the screen, and I felt my gut leap, the butterfly/nausea thing at work again. But this time it came along with a dizziness and double vision. I closed my eyes to answer.

"You're awake!" Stan sounded relieved. "Jorjana and David have been keeping me posted. I'm glad nothing was broken, but you have a dislocated shoulder?"

I gave him a quick update on my aches and pains, but I couldn't offer much information about how I spent my night after leaving Sosei. Much of that was a little fuzzy. But my memory was plenty clear regarding the events that had led up to my injury.

"What happened to Francis?" I asked. I could tell from the exhaustion in his voice that he had been up all night. Surely the cops knew what had happened by now.

Stan didn't answer right away. I wasn't too out of it to realize that wasn't a good sign.

"Stan? Do you know what happened?" I asked again.

"Just a minute," he replied. I heard him mutter something to someone, and then a door closed. Footsteps across a wood floor and then the crunch of gravel. A car door opened and shut, and Stan came back on the line.

"I'm still at the scene," he said. "It looks to me like you interrupted a burglary in progress, but I gotta tell you the Homicide guys are not so sure."

"Not so sure about what?"

"Not so sure you didn't have something to do with it."

"That's ridiculous! You told them that, right?"

"I did, but they know about our relationship, so they didn't pay much attention to my opinion." There was just a hint of irritation in Stan's voice at that.

"I have a meeting with those guys in about an hour. Why do they think I had something to do with…this?" I couldn't bring myself to say "murder." It was hard enough to just think about it.

"They have to eliminate the possibility that you intended to rob Francis and killed her in a struggle."

"But I was attacked too!"

It's just a possibility that they have to follow."

"How can they even think that? I was knocked out! I—"

"Calm down, Alana. They're just doing their job. Remember, no one saw you being knocked out. David and Meredith found you hiding in the bathroom with Francis's body."

Well, that was true. It occurred to me that my interview with the cops might be anything but a routine questioning. Stan must have read my mind.

"You have a lawyer going with you, right?"

"Yeah, I'm meeting them at Richard Lafferty's house."

"Good. Richard is an ass, but he'll take good care of you."

I knew that only too well, but I saw no reason to let Stan know just how well acquainted I was with Richard Lafferty's law skills. Better just to change the subject.

"You sound exhausted," I told him. "When are you off duty?"

"Right now. I thought I'd go back to your place and crash. Is that OK?"

It was more than OK. It was perfect. I knew Jorjana would insist that I remain under her supervision. After I got done with the cops, all I really wanted to do was go home, crawl into bed, and sleep until I stopped hurting. And I wanted to sleep in my own bed in my own house, where I knew the sounds of things that went bump in the night—and where maids didn't sneak up behind my back wielding cups of coffee. Having Stan in the house with his gun on the nightstand would ease both Jorjana's mind and mine.

My call with Stan ended when David found me and announced that it was time for us to go. Stan told me to do whatever Richard said. We agreed to meet later at my house. A wheelchair appeared with Nurse Terry pushing it. I wasn't about to argue. The front door was at least four miles away from the breakfast room. I gave Jorjana the news about Stan staying at my house, thereby sidestepping the discussion over returning to the York Estate. I gave her a kiss and promised to call her later.

David led the way, and minutes later I was in the backseat of the York Bentley and on my way to talk to the cops. I'd like to say it was the first time I was ever formally questioned by a cop.

I hoped like hell it would be the last.

Chapter Fourteen

MEREDITH

Meredith Mackenzie took a deep breath and told herself everything would work itself out somehow.

Although it was hard to see it at the moment.

The ceiling of Errands, Etc. still lay open to the sky, and Lloyd Evans's roofers were stuck in traffic. Her phone had not stopped ringing since she snuck out of the blissful comfort of the York Estate at 6:00 a.m. Most of her staff had called in to say they would be late. And now David Currie called to say Alana Fox needed someone to hold her hand while she talked to the cops.

"Can't she go by herself, David? We're getting slammed here!" Meredith gritted her teeth and wished she had slugged Alana a little bit harder. Then she chided herself for being a bitch. Alana was injured, and Francis Ferguson was dead.

"Oh, no, darling! She needs me."

"Well, I need you too." Then she hung up before saying something she would have to apologize for and wondered why she was so testy this morning.

Back in the temporary workspace, Meredith found the three employees who had managed to show up: Todd and Phil (the outdoor Christmas-decorating guys) and the new girl, Jenny. The three of them looked at the whiteboard as if it were written in hieroglyphics, which Meredith realized was entirely her fault. David normally filled out the errands in his precise, neat printing. Meredith had been so harried taking down orders from her phone that she had scribbled the information in shorthand that only she could understand.

"I'll clean up that board, guys. You met Jenny?"

Introductions went all around, and Meredith brought them up to speed on the repairs to the roof and carpet. While she set about rewriting the errand board, the phone kept ringing. Todd took the orders and assigned them to employees not yet on site; Phil and Jenny sorted out the mess of supplies; and Meredith remembered why she paid David as much as she did. Which only reminded her that he had abandoned her to babysit Alana Fox. Which made Meredith wish she had just shot Alana when she'd had the chance. Once again she wondered what the hell her problem was.

"Meredith, might I have a moment?"

Lloyd Evans stood in the doorway.

Something about Lloyd always made Meredith feel like a dust-encrusted cow at the end of a long cattle drive. The guy never had a wrinkled anything on him; his hair always had a perfect silver sheen. He never lost his cool either. Meredith never had seen Lloyd so much as raise his voice. Even when she had delivered the bad news about the roof, he had maintained his composure. She had no idea how he did it.

"Meredith, I have good news. The roofing crew has arrived. They will put up a temporary cover that will suffice until the supplies are available to reroof everything. Also I have carpet cleaners on the way. This crew specializes in cleaning up after floods. You should be back in your own offices by evening."

"Good news. Thanks, Lloyd."

"Yes, I knew you would be relieved." Then he took her by the arm and led her outside. He turned to face her, his eyes tearing up.

"I am sick about Francis. She was a dear, dear friend. Please tell me what happened."

Lloyd looked tired, the kind of tired that grief inserts into your soul. Meredith knew that exhaustion only too well. Then she realized what was bothering her this morning. She had spent the last fifteen years keeping her own grief at bay by working hard and never looking back. She wanted to tell the story of finding Francis dead about as much she wanted pull out her teeth with a set of pliers. Better to just get on with life. Better to move forward and not dwell on what couldn't be changed. What was done was done.

But she knew full well that Lloyd needed to know. As awful as it was, there was always the need to know what happened just in case the death could have been prevented. Because feeling guilty was more empowering than feeling helpless.

So she told Lloyd what she knew about Francis's death, beginning with the phone call from Grace to finding Francis's body in the bathroom. As she feared, the retelling brought back the old memories she had worked hard to suppress.

Memories like the discovery her parents hadn't returned from visiting her lousy brother in jail. Memories like the phone call from the county sheriff telling her there had been a car wreck. Memories like identifying her parents' bodies the day before high school graduation. Yeah, those memories.

Lloyd's face paled. Meredith worried that he might faint, and she wasn't feeling strong enough to catch him. Nor did she have the time to revive him. She had work to do. A lot of work was needed to shove the grief and guilt back down where it belonged.

Lloyd closed his eyes and took a deep breath. His color returned, and he opened his eyes. "This is very hard news to hear. I have known Francis for over sixty years. She was a remarkable woman. Very loyal, so devoted to Milton. I had hoped she would have a few years to be herself once he was gone. But now..."

His voice trailed off. He pulled a crisply pressed linen handkerchief from his back pocket and rubbed his eyes. Lloyd returned the handkerchief to his pocket and visibly restored his composure. "Thank you for the information, Meredith. I will stop by and see Grace today. She will likely need help in managing George."

Meredith understood that well enough. George Ferguson was known around Malibu for his bad temperament. The only thing worse than having the man for a client would be having him for a brother. Or stepbrother. Meredith never could keep the Ferguson family tree straight. At any rate the man would be a nightmare to plan a funeral with.

Meredith made a mental note to send Grace one of the grief baskets that Errands did so well. One with lots of wine. She felt her spirits pick up. Once again, having work to do made her feel stronger.

"Life does go on, doesn't it, though?" Lloyd said, switching gears. "Could I have Jenny for another day? She is remarkable with the computer issues. She has cleaned up bugs I didn't even know we had."

Meredith needed Jenny's help with the errands that were pouring in. But then she remembered that Jenny wasn't bonded yet, so she couldn't go into clients' homes. Why wasn't David busy seeing to bonding the new employees instead of pandering to Alana Fox? She added an ass chewing to her list of things to do and felt better.

She ducked her head in the door and called out to Jenny.

"Thank you, Meredith," Lloyd said, as he took Jenny by the arm. "With any luck we will all be up and running normally again by tomorrow."

As Jenny and Lloyd left, Meredith turned her attention to the work at hand, the most pressing of which were hysterical clients needing their Christmas trees decorated in time for Hanukkah. Only in Malibu.

Chapter Fifteen

Richard Lafferty lives on a bluff with the kind of views that you would expect of an attorney who charges a few grand an hour. I'm a regular visitor to Richard's place, not always as a client, so the tight switchback road leading up the hill did not faze me. The chauffeur, however, grimaced as he guided the Bentley around each harrowing turn. David worked his phone like a shoe addict at a Louboutin sale. I lay my head back on the hand-stitched leather seat and wondered whether the spinning sensation I felt was from the pain in my shoulder or the pain-killers. For whatever reason, I felt like hell.

The cops arrived first. Two of them stood at the door, a hand-carved mahogany-and-glass creation that cost more than they both made all year. Richard stood in his doorway, all six foot five of him dressed in a bespoke suit. Beyond Richard I could see through the living room to the infinity pool and the view of the Pacific Ocean. The weather was Malibu perfect: clear blue skies, gentle breezes, and the sun beaming away. On lounge chairs around the pool lay Richard's matching Russian wolfhounds, lazily watching the gardeners clean up the mess left from the storm. A maid scurried to their side and opened a shade umbrella lest the wolfhounds caught sunburn.

I had arrived in a chauffeur-driven Bentley. It occurred to me that the cops would be less than sympathetic.

"Darling, can you manage without me?" asked David, who looked worriedly at his phone. "Meredith is *frantic!* I really must get to Errands."

"Sure. Go ahead."

I suspected the less entourage I brought along the better. David promised to send the chauffeur right back and all but pushed me out of the car. As the Bentley purred away, I walked toward Richard and the cops, with my head spinning, my shoulder aching, my jaw throbbing, and a sense that things would get worse before they got better.

***

Not surprisingly, the cops were skeptical of my story. We sat in Richard's living room, a space best described as "contemporary Asian with a rustic twist." Meaning the place was decorated sparsely with minimalist furniture. A two-story tall fireplace was surrounded by river rock, and a life-size blue ceramic Buddha was tucked in a corner. Richard took a chair with his back to the view, a spot that cast a shadow and made it hard to see his face. The cops, one large and one short, took two chairs facing the view. This left me with the sofa, which was long and low and piled high with fur pillows. It was impossible to get comfortable on the contraption. I kept twisting and turning, trying to find a spot to rest my arm, which probably made me look skittish and guilty as hell.

"You're sure you were hit from behind, Mrs. Fox?" asked the short cop.

"Yes. I have a bump on my head, see?" I touched the back of my head and found a lump the size of golf ball.

"How did you get that bruise on your chin?" Large cop.

"Meredith punched me."

"And why did Ms. Mackenzie need to hit you?" Large cop again.

Large and slow on the uptake. By then we had gone over this part of the story at least twice.

The short cop tried another approach. "Are you having financial difficulties, Mrs. Fox?"

"No."

"Why did you lease office space at the Town Center?"

"Because I am expanding my business, and I wanted a professional setting."

"What is it, exactly, that you do?"

"I am a social consultant."

Both cops looked at me like I had donned a tiara and handed them a dance card. In other words they thought I was nuts. Which was probably better than thinking I was guilty.

"I think you gentlemen have covered everything sufficiently." Richard said. "This is obviously a case of a burglary interrupted. I am certain you have a lot of work to do to find the killer. You must be eager to be on your way. As you can see, my client has sustained significant injuries and needs to rest."

He stood to indicate the interview was over.

By my calculations we were ten grand into Richard's fee. I had told the story over and over. As far as I could tell, I told the same story each time. That's a nice feature about the truth; it's easier to keep the story straight.

The cops took the hint. The short one handed me his card and told me to call him if I thought of anything else. The large one glared at Richard. Pleasantries were not exactly exchanged, but the cops left and I wasn't in handcuffs, so I figured the interview had gone well.

Richard had a different opinion.

"Jesus H. Christ, Alana! How the hell do you get into these messes?"

"What are you talking about?"

"You'd better say your prayers that the autopsy doesn't come back with your hair or tissue anywhere on Francis. The cops can make a case that she hit you trying to defend herself."

"But Meredith hit me! And David was there!"

Richard looked at me the way one would regard a twelve-year-old who still believed in the tooth fairy.

"Meredith didn't hit you on the back of the head, Alana."

"Neither did Francis, Richard."

I was on my feet then, stretched up to my full five feet four inches and pissed off enough to tower over him emotionally. "I did not kill Francis. If you don't believe me, I will hire someone who does."

I must have raised my voice, because the wolfhounds looked up from their chaises and growled. Richard gave a hand signal that stopped the growling, but both dogs trained their eyes on me.

"I believe you, Alana. I need you to understand that until the police arrest someone, you will remain a person of interest. As such you'd better behave in a manner that does not arouse suspicion. *Do* you understand?"

"Yeah, I get it. Be a good girl; don't interfere with the police investigation."

Richard seemed appeased, but he looked at me with concern, and this time it wasn't because of something he was afraid I would do.

"You're staying at the Yorks', right?"

"No, I'm going home tonight. Why?"

"Is that cop you're seeing staying with you?"

"His name is Stan, and I don't see how any of that is your business."

"It is my business because you are my client. I don't want you to be alone until whoever killed Francis is arrested."

"You don't think he's going to come after me, do you?"

"You're a witness in a murder investigation, Alana," Richard said. "We don't know who we're dealing with. Just promise me you won't be alone."

I promised. And did my best to keep my panic intact.

"Call me if those two cops show up again," Richard said. "You know where to reach me."

Yes, I did. Richard Lafferty was number three on my speed dial.

***

Back in the Bentley, the chauffeur asked where I preferred to go. I told him to take me home. I was tired, my head ached, my shoulder hurt, my jaw was sore, and I now was scared out of my wits. All I wanted was to lock the bolts on my doors and lie in my own bed and sleep for a year. After I made sure Stan's gun was loaded.

Halfway down the hill, I changed my plans. I remembered I had friends who were having a tougher day than me. I managed to get my cell phone out of my bag and dialed Grace McDonald.

Ten minutes later the chauffeur let me off in front of the McDonald house. Or at least as close as he could get. The driveway was clogged with vehicles: cars, delivery vans, and a lone truck belonging to an aquarium service. I made my way to the front door just as Todd from Errands, Etc. emerged from the house.

"Hey, there Mrs. Fox," Todd said. "How ya doin'?" He eyed my sling with sympathy.

"Fine, thanks."

"Sorry about your shoulder. I did the same thing playing football. Hurts like hell, doesn't it? Gotta go." He sprinted away.

Yeah, it did hurt like hell. I wondered whether I could sneak into Grace's wine cellar without being noticed. I've learned a nice Cabernet can dull just about anything.

I never made it to the wine cellar. I set one foot inside the door, and Grace was all over me.

"Alana, thank you for coming!"

Grace broke away from a crowd of people gathered around the dining table. Gift baskets, floral arrangements, and the inevitable array of casseroles occupied the table and flowed out into the kitchen. I recognized the largest basket as the Errands, Etc. grief arrangement—a lovely selection of comfort foods including a ham, cornbread muffins, and a pecan pie. There appeared to be a few extra bottles of wine tucked inside. I gave silent kudos to Meredith Mackenzie and wondered whether one of the bottles was a nice Cab.

Grace wore a long linen tunic over leggings and was barefoot. Her hair flew wildly around her face. Her eyes were red. She looked as exhausted as I felt. She hugged me ever so gently, and I felt her hold back a sob.

"Grace, I am so sorry," I said. The words weren't nearly compassionate enough. But then do words ever make the grief go away?

"This is so awful. I still can't believe it." Grace dabbed her eyes with a handkerchief. "Let's find a quiet place where we can talk. Mark wants to see you too."

Mark Ferguson, Grace's younger brother, left the crowd at the table and followed us down a set of stairs outside. The weather had cleared, and the sun shone, but it was still chilly. Grace led us to the pool area behind the house. Next to the pool was a gazebo that covered a seating area with fire pit burning invitingly.

Grace took the time to see that I was seated comfortably with a pillow to support my arm and a blanket to ward off any chill. She sat next to Mark and linked her arm in his. As they sat side by side, there was no mistaking they were siblings. Both had Milton Ferguson's long legs and solid build. From Francis they had inherited striking light-blue eyes and thick hair. They seemed to lean into each other for support as if singularly they would topple over from grief.

"Alana, I heard you were hurt, but I had no idea how badly." Mark looked at me with concern. "Thank you for coming over."

"Yes. Thank you," Grace added. "Please tell us whatever you can."

So I did. This recollection of the story differed from what I'd relayed to the cops. I told Grace and Mark about their mother's desire to contact her old girlfriends. I told them about the trips to the Hotel del Coronado. I explained Francis's regret over letting the friendships expire. I omitted the part about Francis and Milton's affair. I spent a lot of time talking about how Francis looked, what she ate and how ready she was to start a new chapter in her life. I did my best to make it sound like Francis's last day had been a happy one. As I talked, both Grace and Mark smiled, cried, laughed, and cried some more.

"Mom really could put down the spicy food," Mark said. "She was game for anything. Remember when she took us to the Thai place and ordered everything extra hot?"

"She was the only one who finished her dinner," Grace said with a smile. "We all went home and made sandwiches to keep from starving."

I stopped my story with the lunch at Wasabi. I sensed they wanted to hear the happy stuff, not the gruesome events back at the house.

"Alana, do you have the envelopes Mom gave you?" asked Grace.

They were still in my handbag, where I'd stashed them at lunch. I pulled them out and handed them to her.

"Dot Derringer, Pat Scott, Celeste Monte." Grace examined the front and back of each envelope. "Mark, do you remember hearing Mom mention these women?"

"No, but then she never talked much about her life before Dad—other than the fact that she moved out here from the Midwest and got a job as a seamstress. Funny, I never questioned her about it. I guess that was because Dad's life was so much bigger."

"I know. Everything was always about Dad."

Grace said this in a matter-of-fact voice, not disapproving, not critical. Just a fact of their family's life.

Milton Ferguson had been one of those larger-than-life personalities. He was the kind of man who walked into a room and all the light shone on him. He worked on a big scale; his successes and failures were legendary. He had friends or enemies and no one in between. Francis was the calm presence in that dynamic—steady, reliable. I could see how she might pale in comparison.

Grace and Mark handed the envelopes back and forth. Then they looked at each other, and some sort of silent sibling agreement passed between them. Grace gave the envelopes back to me.

"Alana, contacting these women was our mother's last wish. Would you please honor it for us?"

Of course I would.

I had told Francis I would track down her friends for her, and I intended to keep that promise. I told Grace and Mark this. As soon as I could drive again, I'd get right on it. Likely the next week.

"But I want them to come to Mom's memorial," Grace protested. "We're planning it for Monday."

"I doubt I'll be able to drive…"

"Then I will drive you myself," Grace said in a tone that didn't leave room to argue. "Can you contact these women and schedule a time to visit them?"

What was I going to say? Some of my comforting words to her had been "Is there anything I can do?" Usually everyone just said, "Thank you" and "No." Not that I didn't want to help find Francis's friends. I just didn't want to do it until I felt better. But Grace wouldn't let me off the hook. She said she was available anytime Thursday or Friday. Mark agreed to take the lead in planning the memorial. The two of them were quietly but strongly insistent.

Then it occurred to me that Dot, Pat, and Celeste were Grace and Mark's last ties to Francis. Of course they wanted to meet these women. I told myself to buck up and double the pain meds. I told Grace I would set up the appointments.

As we stood to say our good byes, George Ferguson blew in out of nowhere.

"There you are! I've been looking everywhere for you two!"

Once again I was struck by how different George was from his half/step/whatever-they-were siblings. It was like comparing a badger with two doves. He stormed toward us, waving a phone in his hand, steam all but blowing out of his nostrils.

"The cemetery wants to confirm the details," George growled. "I told them to talk to you. She wasn't my mother."

"Stop it!" Grace cried. "She was as much your mother as she was ours."

"George, don't start now," Mark pleaded. He took the phone out of George's hands and stepped away, talking calmly to whoever was on the other end.

"She was not my mother! And I am not going to get stuck paying for the service."

"Do we have to discuss this now?" Grace asked. "I'm sure she made provisions in her will for a memorial service."

I made a quick escape. Back in the Bentley, I told the driver to take me home. Now I really had had enough for one day.

Chapter Sixteen

The ride home took about five times as long as it should have. PCH was down to one lane, and there was a detour that I swear took us to Florida and back. I made the most of the time by tracking down Francis's old friends. It did seem odd to me that Francis had their full addresses but no phone numbers. Or maybe she did have the numbers, but we never got around to talking about it. Thinking about how her time had been cut short made me all the more determined to follow through with her wishes.

I found the numbers easily enough, and I left messages for each of the old girlfriends. By the time the Bentley pulled up to my house, I'd heard back from two of them. Dot Derringer had time to see me the next day. Celeste Monte had time the following day. Neither of them sounded happy about it. I got hold of Grace and arranged to have her pick me up at ten the next morning. By then I was so exhausted, I could barely get out of the car.

The chauffeur helped me down the stairs at the front of my house, rang the doorbell, and stood at my side until Stan opened the door. I knew the driver was following Jorjana's instructions to the letter. I'd be lying if I said I found the attention annoying.

Stan planted a kiss on my lips that made the world all right for just a moment.

"I'm so glad to see you," I said with a sigh. "What's that yummy smell?"

"I'm reheating my almost world-famous beef stew," Stan said. "I hope you're hungry. You know I like to cook big."

That was an understatement if ever there was one. On the stovetop was a pot big enough to wash a dog in. I know this because once upon a time I had a dog, and that was what I bought the pot for. The stew simmered merrily away as a batch of biscuits browned in the oven. A giant bouquet of roses sat on the breakfast bar. Best of all, a bottle of Cabernet was opened, flanked by two glasses.

"You're the best. This day has been awful." I sat at the bar and kicked off my shoes. Never had I been more relieved to be home. The yawning hole where my deck once stood didn't even bother me. I was sitting in my own kitchen with my very own cop to protect me and a brand-new bottle of wine to drink. I nearly moaned in gratitude.

"How are you feeling?" Stan looked at my sling with concern. He gently touched my face as he inspected the bruise. He didn't wince, but he didn't look happy with what he saw.

"I'm sore. I'm tired. And I can't believe what happened." I was exhausted from the inside out.

"It'll take a while to get over this," Stan said.

Just then the timer went off on the oven. I shrieked like the thing had hit me from behind.

"Whoa!" Stan grabbed my hand. "What's the matter?"

Everything was the matter.

Which was just what I blabbered out as he let go of my hand to take the biscuits out of the oven. I didn't stop there. Once I got started, my account of my day spewed out as fast as I could think. I told him about the Homicide guys and their insipid questions. I complained about how much my shoulder hurt. I told him what Richard had said about not being alone. I told him how hard it was to eat. I went on and on about how belligerent George Ferguson was. By the time I laid out the details of my day, tears ran down my face.

Believe me, tears do not come easily to me.

"Oh, baby. You are a mess." Stan helped me from the breakfast bar to the comfy couch in the living room. He settled me in, with pillows to support my arm, just like Grace had. He sat next to me and stroked my hair. I finally felt safe enough to let my feelings go.

I cried for Francis. I cried because I was hurt. I cried because I was scared. I cried because my deck was gone. I cried because I was crying and I do not cry. Hardly ever.

Stan whispered in my ear all the way through my meltdown. He promised to take care of me. He said I would be better in time. He said he would stay with me. He promised the police would catch the guy and put him in jail.

Then he ruined everything and said he loved me.

That was the last thing I needed to hear.

Declarations of love should come with sunsets over the Pacific and a chilled bottle of Champagne on the table. You want to hear those words when your makeup is perfect, your hair is bouncy, and you're wearing your skinny clothes. There should be violin music in the background and a little blue box from Tiffany's nearby. That's the way it should be.

Don't tell me you love me when I spent the last half hour sobbing my eyes out, when my arm is in an ugly sling and I can't brush my own hair.

I took one look at him and sobbed. Big, juicy sobs punctuated with hiccups. I was one big blubbering mess with a nasty bruise on my jaw.

Stan, to his credit, held me closer and said, "Lousy timing, I know. But I've been crazy worrying about you. We can talk about this later." He made everything better by asking, "Can you have a glass of wine?"

I knew damn well I couldn't. Or shouldn't. But I needed to drink something to stop the hiccups. So I told him one glass wouldn't hurt anything. I actually believed it too.

Stan got up and poured two generous glasses of Cabernet. When his back was to me, I pulled the pain meds out of my pocket and snuck one in my mouth.

Yeah, I know I shouldn't have.

Well, I know that now. Stan sat next to me; we clinked our glasses in a toast; and that's all I remember about Wednesday.

****

Thursday morning I awoke to clear blue skies and a massive headache. I also woke up in my bed with no recollection of how I got there.

I took a quick inventory. My head hurt. My shoulder felt better. I was wearing the clothes from yesterday. I was alive. The sun was shining. But Stan was nowhere to be seen. So much for his undying love.

I rolled over to my good shoulder and spotted a note on the pillow next to me.

Good morning, gorgeous. I didn't leave you alone. There's a patrol car outside. Nurse Terry is downstairs, so don't freak out if you hear someone moving around. Call me when you get up. Love, Stan

Love. That again.

Sooner or later I would have to decide how to respond. Like I didn't have enough to worry about.

I rolled back over. This time it hurt. I moaned. I reached for the pain meds in my pocket. They were gone.

Nurse Terry peeked her head in from the hall. "How are you feeling, Mrs. Fox?"

I was startled even though I knew she was in the house. With my heart thumping, I tried to sit up. Big mistake. Pain shot through my arm and out my fingers. Again.

"Let me help you."

Nurse Terry was at my side in an instant, working her magic to get me on my feet. She helped me to the bathroom and pointed out the window at the patrol car parked in front. She gave me a pain pill then put the bottle back in her own pocket. She got me in the shower, helped me dress, and dried my hair. By the time she brushed some blush on my cheeks, I was feeling well enough to recognize a conspiracy.

"When did Stan and Jorjana arrange all this?" I asked.

"Last night. Mrs. York and Mr. Sanchez are worried about you. You need to rest today. I'm here to help you, and the police are outside to keep you safe. You have nothing to worry about."

Nothing like having your life kidnapped by good intentions.

I did appreciate what Jorjana and Stan were trying to do. I did ask for their help, so Jorjana sent Terry to Alana-sit, and Stan planted cops at my door. I knew they cared about my well-being, and for that I was grateful. But I felt so much better. There was no way in hell I was going to stay cooped up in my house all day long while Nurse Terry popped out of nowhere to scare the wits out of me.

I told Terry I needed to make some phone calls from my library. She got me downstairs and settled at my desk. I sent her off in search of toast and coffee. Then I set about regaining control of my life.

Maybe it was the good night's sleep. Maybe it was my natural stubbornness to do things myself. Maybe it was my loyalty to Francis's memory. But once the pain meds got rid of my aches, I was ready to take on the things I had said I would do. I pride myself on always following through.

But first I had to get Jorjana and Stan out of my way.

My first call was to Jorjana.

"Alana! How are you feeling this morning?" Jorjana sounded delighted to hear my voice.

"I'm much better. Thanks for sending Terry over, but I'm going to send her back to you in a little bit. I've got an errand to run with Grace today."

That went over about as badly as I'd anticipated. It took some back-and-forth negotiation, but eventually I convinced Jorjana that I was well enough leave the house for "an hour at most." I had to agree to allow Nurse Terry to wait for me to return, and I had to promise to keep an appointment with a doctor that David had arranged. I told Jorjana I'd call her later in the day and hung up before she thought to have a tracking device attached to my ankle.

The phone call to Stan went directly to message and spared me a new set of promises I had no intention of keeping.

"I'm awake," I said to Stan's voice mail. "I'm feeling a lot better, and Terry's making breakfast for me as I speak. Thanks for the patrol car, but I'm going out with Grace later today so they don't need to stick around here. I'll call you later."

I hung up and fired up my computer as Terry delivered perfectly toasted toast and freshly brewed coffee. With a tummy fueled on toast and my head cleared by caffeine, I checked my e-mails. There were only about a million. I sat back with the coffee cup in hand and sighed. On my desk sat a stack of invitations for dinner parties, gallery openings, dance parties, and all the events that make up the holidays. I put the coffee cup down and used my one good hand to open the calendar on my computer. Jorjana's social secretary had done what he could to rearrange my schedule into the next week. With any luck, if I found an extra nine hours in each day, I would be able to accommodate all requests for my time with no problem. Assuming, of course, I had the use of both arms and an army of elves set up my new office space.

I had no time for self-pity. A honk outside told me Grace McDonald had arrived.

Chapter Seventeen

Grace stood outside her Cadillac Escalade, talking to the cops. She stood as if it took all of her energy. Her hair was limp, her eyes puffy.

I gave her a hug. Then I tried to tell the cops I didn't need their assistance. It was like trying to talk to a couple of tree stumps. They had their orders. They would follow us. I explained that we were headed out of LA County to Camarillo. That gave them pause, but they insisted they would follow even to the depths of Ventura County. I didn't have the energy to argue. With Grace's help I climbed into the Escalade, and we were on our way.

Camarillo is a bedroom community northeast of Malibu. It is a pleasant half-hour drive under normal conditions. Just cruise north on PCH, and enjoy watching dolphins cavorting in the surf. But that too had changed with the storms and the resulting mudslides. PCH north was closed. Our trek to Camarillo would take a good hour on a circuitous route.

"What's with the police protection?" Grace asked once we were underway.

"It's Stan's way of keeping an eye on me." I told her about the meeting with the Homicide guys and Richard's advice to me about not being alone.

"Those Homicide detectives are idiots," Grace said. "When they talked to me, they kept asking about your financial status. To be honest, when I saw the cops outside your house, I thought they were following you, not protecting you."

"Stan arranged for them. They're for protection."

As I said it, I had a momentary doubt. Were the cops really suspicious of me? What if they had jumped at the chance to follow me under the guise of protecting me?

I told myself to calm down and not let my imagination run away. I wondered whether a side effect of alcohol and pain meds was paranoia. Then I told myself to knock it off. I wasn't the only one in the car with problems.

"How are you doing, Grace?" I asked.

"I'm numb. I'm in shock," she said. "I have this weird obsession to keep moving. Mark really has a need to plan the memorial service, so I don't want to get in his way. I'm actually glad I have an errand to run. I'm afraid that if I stop moving I'll collapse."

"You need to rest at some point," I said, like I listened to that advice myself.

"I will. Just not yet."

"Alana, I have to apologize for George's behavior yesterday," Grace said as if to change the subject. "He's upset and doesn't have the sense to watch what he says. His relationship with Mom was always strained. I've spent my whole life wishing things were different between them."

"Your mom told me that George was adopted," I said. "I always thought he was your father's son from a first marriage."

With a long drive ahead, perhaps I finally would sort out the twisted branches of the Ferguson family tree. And keep my mind off the motivations of the cops following us.

"I've always considered George my half-brother," Grace explained. "Dad's first wife was a woman named Lydia Attel. She came from old Pasadena money, orange groves or something. They met on the studio lot when Dad was just starting out. Lydia was an actress. I've seen pictures of her; she was stunning. Dad and Lydia had a child that was stillborn, and apparently Lydia took it hard. Dad tried making things better by adopting a baby. That was George. Unfortunately Lydia got tuberculosis and died when George was still a toddler. Her family took care of George while Dad was single. George lived with the Attels during the week, and Dad took him on the weekends. George hated it when the Attels sent him back to live with Dad and Mom after they married. George remembers that like it was yesterday, by the way, and he couldn't have been more than two at the time. He made such a stink about it that Dad arranged for George to spend summers with the Attels. In my opinion that was a mistake. George lorded his connection to the Attels over Mark and me all the time."

"Sounds like a stressful childhood," I said.

"It had its ups and downs. Mom kept George in line pretty well when she was home, but she traveled with

Dad often. George could be a real jerk when he had the chance."

She paused, considering something. "You know, I really think George's problem is that he doesn't feel he belongs anywhere. He wasn't a blood relative to the Attels or the Fergusons. I guess that's why he has that chip on his shoulder."

"Could be," I said. Personally I thought George was just a natural-born jerk.

We made it to Dot Derringer's house in just under an hour. Dot lived in a Camarillo housing development that had seen better days. Chain link fences separated row after row of identical stucco houses. The streets were named after trees: Maple, Oak, Acorn, Fir. Dot lived at the corner of Willow and Birch in a white house with a one-car garage and bars on the windows. Her entire lot was smaller than Jorjana's master bathroom.

Grace pulled into the driveway, and the cops parked across the street. We rang the doorbell just on time. From inside the house, a dog barked, and a voice called out, "I'm coming! Quiet, LuLu!"

Dot Derringer had seen better days. She was a husky woman of medium height and large girth. Her hair was one of those teased-and-sprayed creations only a hair salon has a license to build. She wore a garment best described as a housecoat of many colors. She wore it over black stirrup pants, and her feet were stuffed into red sequined ballet slippers. She had matching red sequined earrings and brilliant red fingernails. Suffice it to say that her makeup was as understated as her dress. At her feet bounced a little black-and-white dog.

"Which one of you is Frannie's girl?" Dot started out. "Sit still, LuLu!"

LuLu sat. Sat right down on her haunches and glared up at Dot like she had been insulted.

"That's me. I'm Grace McDonald. It's a pleasure to meet you Mrs. Derringer."

Dot Derringer regarded Grace with suspicion. Looked her up and down. Ignored Grace's outstretched hand when she spotted the patrol car. Then her sights landed on my bruised face and sling. I thought for a second that Dot was going to slam the door in our faces. But then she looked straight into Grace's eyes and visibly relaxed.

"Well, you got your mother's looks for sure. Good thing too, since your dad wasn't that pretty. Come on in. Come, LuLu!"

We followed Dot into her living room. It wasn't a far walk. Dot's house was the kind where the front door opens right into the house. No foyer, no landing. Just open the door and let the living begin.

Or let something begin. Dot's house was filled from floor to ceiling with stuff known as "collectibles." The walls were lined with bookshelves. The shelves held everything but books: metal lunchboxes, troll dolls, sets of dishware that gas stations used to give out. Nearly every pop-culture gadget, game, or freebie was displayed around Dot's living room.

More bookshelves lined a hallway that led to the back of the house. The hallway wasn't that wide to begin with, and the shelving made the passage even narrower. I wondered how Dot maneuvered her girth to the bedroom.

Just beyond the living area was a room originally intended as a dining room. On the table were four computers and at each one sat a Hispanic woman. The computers appeared to be logged into sites like eBay or Etsy, and the women were busily monitoring the activity on each site.

"I work out of my house," Dot said by way of explanation. "Set yourselves down. I made ice tea." Dot waddled off.

Grace and I looked around for a place to "set." In the middle of the room was a small couch facing two dainty chairs. Between them was a plexiglass cube that displayed vintage magic equipment. I remembered Francis saying Dot had married a magician.

I doubted the chairs would withstand Dot's heft, so I set myself on one of them. Grace followed my lead and sat on the other. LuLu hopped onto the couch and settled herself on a satin pillow.

The activity in the dining room was constant. Every few minutes one of the women got up and retrieved an invoice from a central printer. Then she wandered around the house, invoice in hand, before returning with an item. She prepared the item for shipping by putting it in a box, scooping out a handful of Styrofoam popcorn from an aluminum garbage can, securing the box with tape, then weighing it on the scale. A shipping label was applied, and the box went on top of a pile. Then the woman returned to her computer. In the short time that Dot was fetching iced tea, I saw four things readied to ship.

"Don't mind the ladies here. They got their work to do."

Dot came back carrying a tray with glasses of tea and a plate of cookies. The cookies appeared homemade, the kind that have a whole lot of ingredients that aren't good for you but are too damn tasty to resist. Dot rested the tray on the plexiglass cube.

"Here's some tea for you. I have extra sugar if you need it." She handed each of us a glass then offered the cookies. Sadly I had to pass on a cookie since I only had free use of my left hand.

Dot settled herself into the couch and broke off a piece of cookie for LuLu. The dog got up from her pillow to accept the cookie as daintily as you please. Then she returned to the pillow, lay down, and placed the cookie between her paws. She kept her eyes on Dot.

"You can eat it now," Dot said to her. LuLu gobbled up the cookie, and I swear she smiled afterward.

"She's a Havanese," Dot said. "I got her cheap because she's smaller than most. Smart as a whip, though. Good company too. Spoiled rotten, but I got no one to blame but myself on that. I'm real sorry about your mom, Grace. Frannie and me were real close when we were young. She was a good woman."

"Thank you, Mrs. Derringer," Grace said. "Did Alana tell you why we wanted to see you today?"

"Yeah, she said something about a letter from Frannie?"

"Yes, why don't we let Alana tell you the whole story?"

So I did. I was beginning to feel I could retell the story in my sleep. Dot listened intently, her face registering skepticism, tension, then alarm. But she didn't say anything until I finished.

Then she was quiet, deep in thought. If her face were a movie screen, it would have shown every emotion. I saw joy, sadness, then anger parade across her face in the span of a moment.

"Let me read that letter you got," Dot said.

As I handed it to her, something inside the envelope slid around and settled into a corner. Dot produced a pair of bright-red glasses out of the depths of her housecoat. She held the envelope in both hands and peered at the writing as if it were about to talk to her. Then she opened it and pulled out the letter. A small old-fashioned gold key attached to a gold chain slid out from the pages and landed in Dot's lap.

Grace gasped. "That's the key to Mom's heart!" Noticing our confusion, she explained. "Mom wore that all the time. She said she kept it close to her heart because it was the key to it."

I thought Grace's explanation was charming. Dot, however, paled visibly. Her hands shook as she read the letter. When she finished, she carefully folded the paper and returned it to the envelope. She held the key tightly in her hand as she stared at Grace.

"What did your ma tell you about me?"

"Nothing. I first heard of you when Alana told me what Mom wanted to do."

"She never talked about what she did before she married your Dad?"

"No. Mom kept her past pretty much to herself."

"Hmmph." Something clearly was on Dot's mind, and she struggled to sort it out. "Can you girls give me a lift over to my bank? There's something there that Frannie wanted you to see."

"Can't you tell us—" Grace started.

"No, you have to see it. I ain't gonna tell you what it is, but you can read the letter while I find my coat."

Dot gave Grace the envelope as she left the room. Grace opened the letter and leaned over to show me.

Dearest Dot,

I have never forgotten you or how much you did for me when I needed help the most. I regret not being as good a friend to you as you were to me.

Milton has been gone a year now. I kept my promise to him while he was alive. I often questioned if his way was the best for us after all. Now that he is gone, I feel I am released from my pledge. I have decided to tell the truth. You know what this key is for. I apologize for not giving this letter to you in person. It appears that I am still a coward. You were right all along.

Alana Fox, the lovely woman who is delivering this for me, is a dear friend of my daughter, Grace. Please let Alana know if you are willing to see me.

I also have asked Alana to contact Celeste and Pat. It is my fondest wish that I repair the hurts and that we spend that weekend at the Hotel del Coronado that we planned so long ago. Just the four of us, like old times. The Tom Collinses are on me!

With all my love and gratitude,
Frannie

"What does this mean?" Grace asked me. 'Released from my pledge'?"

"It sounds like Dot is keeping one hell of a secret."

I suspected Dot knew that Francis and Milton had an affair while he was still married to his first wife. I have to admit, I was secretly relieved that I didn't have to drop that bombshell on Grace. Why we had to go to the bank was beyond me.

"That key seems to mean something to her," I said. "Are you sure your mother never mentioned any of these friends to you?"

"Never," Grace said with certainty. "She was very evasive about her childhood. She said her life began when she met Dad. He had so many great stories about his life. Whenever a question came up about Mom's past, she changed the subject."

Dot returned wearing a wrinkled white coat that looked like she had pulled a sheet off a bed and wrapped it around herself. She carried a handbag slightly smaller than a suitcase. LuLu trotted at her heels, tail wagging, excited as all get out.

"Let's go," Dot said. "LuLu, you stay here."

LuLu was displeased with this pronouncement. She plopped down on her little hindquarters and glared at Dot.

"We'll be right back," Dot said to her. "Get up on your pillow, and be a good girl."

LuLu stayed plopped. If she could talk, the little dog would have given us an earful.

The ladies in the dining room stayed glued to their computer screens.

Somehow we got Dot into the Escalade without calling for a forklift. I climbed into the middle of the backseat, and Grace put the key in the ignition.

"Why are the cops here?" Dot asked.

"Whoever killed Francis is still on the loose," I said. "The police are protecting me."

Dot let that settle in then gave Grace the directions to the bank. She turned in her seat and gave Grace a long, hard look. "You do favor your mother. She never let on about her life before Milton, huh? All these years, and she never said nothin'?"

"Very little actually." Grace said. "How did you know her?"

"Your ma and me go way back. I met her when she was working in the costume department at the studio. She was one of the seamstresses, and I was a dancer. This was when movies had glamour, not like the crap they make now. We had costumes with sequins and satin and real handmade bows. Real works of art, I tell ya. Your ma and all the other gals worked their fingers to the bone making those costumes. Sometimes we had as many as three fittings for one outfit. It took a lot of time, and being young gals, we giggled our way through it. Your ma and me took a liking to each other. She was rooming with Pat Scott, and I was rooming with Celeste, so we all would go out on the town together. Had some real fun, believe you me."

"Like going to San Diego?" Grace asked.

"That was a real highlight," Dot smiled. "We were so young and had such big dreams." She sighed with the kind of bittersweet longing a good memory brings about.

"Why did you grow apart?"

Dot's face hardened. "There's a lot to that story. Let's see how it goes at the bank."

We rode the rest of the way in silence. On arrival at the bank, Dot produced a handicapped placard for Grace to hang from her rearview mirror. The cops pulled in next to us. We off-loaded Dot with hardly any grunting and groaning. We followed her into the bank, where the bank manager greeted her personally.

"Good morning, Mrs. Derringer," he said. "How can we help you today?"

"Good morning, Mr. Temple. I want to get into my safe-deposit box, and these ladies are coming with me."

The manager was only too happy to help. He ushered us into a private conference room featuring an oval table and six upholstered chairs. Offered coffee. Saw that Grace and I were comfortable and then took

Dot off to fetch the safe-deposit box. She was back in a moment, the manager right behind her, lugging a large metal box. This wasn't one of the small, shallow safe-deposit boxes; it was one of the deep, $350-a-month kind. He set the box on the table and quietly closed the door behind him.

The room was so quiet, you could have heard a dollar bill drop. Dot opened the box and lifted out an antique wooden box, intricately carved and decorated with decoupage. A shiny gold lock held it shut. Dot unlocked the lock with Francis's gold key. She gave the key to Grace and opened the box. A musty smell filled the room. From the box, Dot pulled out a sheet of paper, yellowed and folded in three. She handed it to Grace.

"Your mother was supposed to destroy this, but she didn't have the heart. She asked me to keep it for her. She locked this wooden box herself, and it hasn't been opened since. I've had it in a safe-deposit box for over fifty years. When she said that key was to her heart, she meant it was the key to a secret she kept in her heart all these years."

Grace unfolded the paper. I leaned over to see, being nosy like I am.

The paper was a birth certificate dated November 2, 1946 for the live birth of a baby boy in San Diego, California. Mother was one Francis Martin. Father was one Milton Ferguson. Baby was named George Milton Ferguson.

You could have heard Grace's gasp on the moon.

Chapter Eighteen

"That's right. George Ferguson is your full-blood brother," Dot said. "I know it's true. I was right there when he was born."

"But how? Why?" Grace's face was white.

Having known about the affair, I wasn't so shocked. A little surprised maybe, but nothing a drink couldn't have straightened out. I wondered whether the bank manager kept a stash in his desk drawer.

Dot, as promised, told the story.

"Your dad and ma met in forty-five or so. He was producing one of those propaganda movies for the war effort, and he was a real stickler for details. He hounded those poor girls in the costume department to get every little thing just right. Your ma just knew from the get-go how to handle him. They fell for each other. Lord knows, I told her he was trouble. He was still married to that lunatic Lydia Attel. Spoiled? And a raving bitch— pardon my French. Anyway, your ma and dad fell in love. Then Frannie ends up pregnant. As if that weren't bad enough, Lydia was pregnant too. I told Frannie, I said, that Milton Ferguson is a two timing…"

Dot saw the look on Grace's face and changed her tactic.

"Anyway, I told her not to tell Milton, to just go away and have the baby and give it up and start over somewhere else. But she didn't listen. She went running to Milton, and like I thought, it just got worse."

"But Dad adopted George. How can you adopt your own child?"

Grace clearly was following the story better than me. A nice cold Chardonnay would have helped heaps and heaps.

"I'm getting to that," Dot said. "I'll give Milton this much—he did what he could. Back then unmarried girls went into hiding if they got knocked up. So Milton arranged to have Frannie stay in San Diego until the baby was born. He didn't want her to be alone, so he talked me into going with her. We told everyone we was sisters and she had lost her husband in the war. Milton came down every once in a while, and we said he was my beau. Meanwhile crazy old Lydia is raising hell all through her pregnancy. She had a room added on just for the baby and outfitted it with every fancy thing you could imagine. Her father had more money than God and gave her everything she wanted. Him and Milton butted heads a few times, believe you me. So then Lydia's baby is stillborn. She really goes nuts then. Frannie had her baby about a month later. Then Milton convinces Frannie to give up George to him. I was dead-set against it, and I told Frannie that. But she couldn't bear the thought of never seeing George again, so she gave him up."

"How did Dad explain where he got a baby?" Grace asked.

"Things were different then. Lydia's father was desperate to make his little girl happy. When Milton said he could get his hands on a newborn baby, Mr. Attel was all for it. No questions asked."

"And Mom kept this secret all these years? Who else knew about this?"

"It was just me and your mom and dad and Mr. Attel," Dot said. "The fewer folks who knew, the better."

"You were a very good friend, Dot," Grace said quietly. "Not many would keep a secret this long."

Dot blushed and looked uncomfortable. Instead of "Aw shucks, it was nothing," she looked away.

"I don't know about that," she said quietly. "I couldn't face your ma after all was said and done. I thought she made a big mistake, and I told her as much. And then I needed to get far away from Hollywood and men like Milton Ferguson. I'm sorry to say this to you, Grace, but your dad was one tough son of a bitch. I was scared of him.

"I packed my bags and left for Vegas. I had a friend waiting tables at the Golden Nugget, and she got me a job. I wasn't there two days when one of my customers hands me an envelope. Inside is a letter saying a bank account was opened in my name and fifty thousand dollars was in it. I didn't need any explanations. I knew the money was from Milton, and I was supposed to keep my mouth shut. I wouldn't have said nothing anyway; Frannie was my friend."

"Milton paid you fifty thousand dollars?" Now I was surprised. "That was a lot of money in nineteen forty-six."

Grace and Dot looked at me like I had bats flying out of my head. Obviously I had missed the point.

"It's a lot of money now," Dot said. "I never touched a cent of it. I didn't want to be beholden to Milton Ferguson. I let him think he could buy me, but I never spent his money. And believe you me, there was plenty of times when I could have used that money over the years."

"What did you do with it?" Me, just being nosy.

I peered into the wooden box, half expecting to see a pile of hundred-dollar bills.

Dot pulled a bank statement out of her handbag.

"I kept the account open and just let it build interest."

She showed me the statement. Milton's fifty grand had grown to nearly a quarter of a million even with monthly deductions to pay for the safe-deposit box. No wonder the bank manager was so attentive to Dot.

The business side of me balked at the idea of leaving that kind of money to slowly accrue interest over sixty-five years. I fought back the urge to haul the bank manager in by his ear and demand that he put Dot's money in an interest-bearing bond. But for once I kept my mouth shut.

"You gonna tell George this, or you want me to?" Dot asked Grace. "I heard he was a real pissant to your ma over the years. I sure would like to see the look on his face when he hears she was his real mother."

Grace winced. "I think this is best coming from me."

"You change your mind, you just let me know. I got a few things I'd like to say to that boy."

I could only imagine.

Chapter Nineteen

MEREDITH

Meredith Mackenzie told herself to shut up and let Chanie Bramlette ramble on and on. So she held her cell phone in one hand and covered her mouth with the other.

"And then the director, like, ya know, said we had to shoot the scene over, like, again and…"

The crux of the reality star's problem had something to do with reshooting a bar scene where Chanie ended up in a tussle.

"…and then that bitch, like, socked me and, like, broke my nose! Which is totally awesome 'cuz now the network, like, has to pay for a new nose."

Meredith was convinced that when Chanie had her boobs done, the surgeon simply removed Chanie's brain, sliced it in half, and inserted it in her chest. That would explain a lot, in Meredith's opinion.

"So now I'm, like, coming home early, and they're, like, sending a plane, ya know?"

Meredith snapped to attention at "coming home early." She tried to remember when she had last dropped by to see Chanie's cat. Baby had enough food and water for several days. Didn't she? But who knew what havoc the cat had wreaked while left on its own.

"When are you coming home, Chanie? Do you need us to pick you up?"

"Naw, the network will send a limo to pick me up, ya know? I'll be home, like, tomorrow night. See ya!"

Meredith hung up her cell phone and silently cursed the damn storm. Between the road closures, the roof damage, and the employees who couldn't get into work, Errands, Etc. was days behind schedule. They had spent the better part of the day moving out of Alana Fox's tiny office and back into their original space. At the rate things were going, they wouldn't get their Thanksgiving errands done until New Year's Eve.

She scanned the errand board for tomorrow's errands. Todd and Phil were scheduled to hang Christmas lights. Terry had dozens of gift baskets to assemble. Peggy would be chained to the writing desk, addressing clients' Christmas cards in her exquisite calligraphy. Everyone else had to deliver/pick up/do/undo.

Meredith fought back a rising panic that everything was piling up too fast. All day she had accepted errand requests and sent out employees in a frenzied rush. She felt like she had spent her day at one of those carnival games where you bat down the groundhogs as soon as they pop up. And things were not likely to lighten up. The errand board was crammed full, straight through to Thanksgiving.

Meredith told herself to knock off acting like one of her hysterical clients. Somehow Errands, Etc. always managed. Somehow decorations went up, baskets were delivered, and kids made it to and from soccer practice in one piece. Some days were just harder than others. Today had felt like she was trapped in a crazy carnival because they were so far behind. And she was still reeling over what had happened to Francis Ferguson.

Meredith turned away from the errand board and walked back to her office. She plopped into her chair, put her feet up on her desk, and told herself she had five minutes to feel badly about Francis, and that was it. Five minutes to let the shock register. Five minutes to address the fear. Five minutes to just get over it and then get on with it.

After five minutes she knew it wasn't enough time. But sitting alone in her tiny office wouldn't make everything better. There were three condolence baskets still to deliver to Grace McDonald's place, and everyone already had gone home. The last errand of the day had landed in her lap.

The last thing Meredith felt like doing was driving all the way down PCH and up the hill to Grace's house then all the way up PCH to Broad Beach to feed the damn cat. But it looked like that was how she would spend her evening.

Then she remembered Jenny Shu. Maybe Jenny could run out and feed the cat in the morning before returning to Lloyd's computer woes.

Meredith paused. She couldn't remember seeing the bonding clearance that would allow Jenny to enter a client's house. David certainly had finished her bonding process. Hadn't he?

As if on cue, Meredith's cell rang. It was David.

"Hello, darling! I mailed the bills at the post office and picked up the Carlsons' Christmas-card list—is there anything else? Because I am spent, darling!"

"I need someone to check on Chanie Bramlette's cat and tidy up her house." Meredith said. "Do you have Jenny Shu's bonding paperwork? I thought I'd send her in the morning."

Silence from David. Never a good sign.

"No, darling. I'm sorry, but there is a hold-up on Jenny's papers."

"What the hell have you been doing?" Meredith barked at him.

More silence. Then David spoke, in full sentences. An even worse sign.

"Darling, Jenny's paperwork seems to be lost in the mix. I will check first thing in the morning. I promise."

For some reason his explanation pissed Meredith off.

"How can it be 'lost in the mix'? How incompetent is our insurance agency? I pay them enough that they should be able to get back to us the same day! How can they lose info on a new employee? How hard is it to check someone's background?"

"I am sure they are overwhelmed with processing claims from the storm damage. I waited nearly an hour the other day for Alana's agent to get back to me. This is not like you. What is bothering you, darling?"

Meredith knew, deep down, that she was out of line. But something about David's effort to calm her down pissed her off even more.

"What I need is for *all* my employees to be available when I need them. Is that so hard to do?"

"No, it is not. I will personally stop by the insurance agency in the morning and find out what is holding up Jenny's paperwork. If it will help, I will go and check on Chanie's little cat myself."

"Yes, that will help." Meredith felt her frustration ease off just a bit. She dialed the combination to the gun safe and swung open the door. She found the key to Chanie's house and put it in the mug that held her pens on the desk.

"I'll leave the key in the mug."

David was silent a moment more. When he responded, his voice was controlled, and he still spoke in full sentences. "I'll come in early and grab the key. Then I will take care of the cat and tidy up the house. And I will stop by the insurance agency and see what the hold-up is." A deliberate pause and then, "You might want to clean up that little attitude of yours, missy. I *am* on your side, you know."

Meredith was decent enough to feel the sting of his words. But she was stubborn enough not to offer up an apology.

"Let me know the minute you hear from the insurance guys."

She wasn't sure who hung up on whom.

***

The circular drive in front of the McDonalds' home was packed. Meredith recognized Grace's Escalade and her brother Mark's Range Rover. George Ferguson's flashy red Corvette and an assortment of cars she knew belonged to Grace's boys spilled out of the driveway and into the street.

Meredith parked her truck down the hill and double-checked that her brake was set and her wheels curbed. She grabbed the gift baskets and decided it was best not to interrupt the family. She took a path on the side of the house that she knew led to a door on the lower level. Using a key she'd retrieved from the safe in her office, she quietly let herself in.

The door opened to the media room, which featured a projection screen and a sectional sofa slightly smaller than a football field. Sprawled around the sofa were Mark's wife and kids, Grace's five grown sons, Grace's three daughters-in-law, and a herd of Grace's grandchildren. The movie *Mary Poppins* played on the screen to the rapt attention of the kids and the boredom of the adults.

One of Grace's sons waved a hand in greeting as Meredith entered the room.

Another son looked at the baskets in her arms and pointed up the stairs.

Mark's wife said, "Good luck. They're in the living room."

No one made a move to help her.

Meredith paused. The main level of the McDonald house was one open room. She wasn't sure how she could get into the kitchen without interrupting whatever "they" were doing.

Shifting the baskets so she could see where she was going, she climbed the staircase as Julie Andrews sang "A Spoonful of Sugar." Meredith intended to tiptoe to the kitchen table, drop the baskets off, and tiptoe out. Halfway up she understood why Mark's wife had wished her good luck.

"Now George, I know this is a shock, but—" Grace said.

"I don't believe it! I *won't* believe it!" George shouted. "Who is this woman anyway? Did you ever hear Francis talk about her?"

"Well, no, but there was so much about Mother's life that we didn't—"

"She's after something! She wants money, doesn't she? We'll just see..."

"She doesn't want anything from us, George," Grace said, sounding like a kindergarten teacher soothing an upset five-year-old. "Mother wanted to reconnect with her, and from the letter, it sounded like she wanted to tell you the truth."

"George, look at this birth certificate," Mark said.

"Anyone can print up a document these days! I could prove you were born on the moon if I wanted! That certificate is fake, and that woman is a crook! I'm calling Lloyd Evans and demand that he get to the bottom of this!"

"Now George..."

"Don't you think..."

Grace and Mark's pleas went unheeded. Meredith heard the front door slam.

"George, come back!"

Meredith stepped up the stairs far enough to see Grace and Mark open the door and race outside after George. The door remained ajar and Meredith saw them stop George in the driveway. She dumped the gift baskets on the kitchen table and scribbled a quick note of explanation. Then she scurried down the stairs as Julie Andrews suggested a spoonful of sugar to help the medicine go down. No one on the couch turned as she went out the door.

As Meredith climbed the path on the side of the house, she heard the argument continue. She stepped behind a hedge to wait for them to finish.

George's face was nearly blue with anger. He stood with his fists clenched. Mark tried to take George's arm, but George wrenched it away then shook his fist at Mark. Grace stepped between them. Meredith held her breath. In her experience the argument was at the tipping point. Either the men would step down or someone was leaving in an ambulance.

Grace straightened her arm up against Mark's chest. Her other hand went on George's shoulder. She leaned into George and appeared to whisper in his ear. George, much to Meredith's relief, stepped away. Grace let go of George's shoulder and turned to Mark. She put her hands on Mark's shoulders and whispered to him. He, in turn, stepped back.

"Tomorrow we'll go and see Lloyd together, agreed?" said Grace.

Mark spun on his heel and stormed back in the house. George flung himself into his Corvette and sped off. Grace sighed and followed Mark inside.

Meredith waited to hear the front door shut before walking back to her truck. It wasn't the first time she had walked in on a family fight. It likely wasn't the last. Fortunately Grace and Mark hadn't seen her. The last thing they needed was to know someone had witnessed the argument. Well, the last thing they needed after losing their mother was a fight with George. Meredith wondered why George was so upset about a birth certificate. It sure had hit a nerve.

She let herself back in the truck, released the brake, and headed home.

***

Meredith's home was a single-wide parked in Paradise Cove, a private reserve of mobile homes built in the embrace of a bluff that overlooked the ocean.

Twelve years ago she used part of her inheritance to buy the place because it offered unobstructed views of the ocean and nothing to remind her of Montana. She paid a ridiculous price for it then. It was worth an even more ridiculous sum now.

She had what she needed to spend a night or two—a hammock in the smaller bedroom and a stool at the kitchen counter. Toiletries in the bathroom. A few towels. A ceramic mug and a coffee pot. She never had bothered to furnish the place because she spent most nights house-sitting in swankier digs.

Meredith tossed her keys on the counter next to the photo of her parents. She dropped her tote bag on the floor and started down the hall to the bathroom. Something made her stop and turn around.

The west wall of her single-wide featured sliding glass doors that opened to a deck. The view stretched over the curved beach of Paradise Cove down to the lights of Pacific Palisades. The spectacular view had convinced her to invest money in a nine-hundred-square-foot trailer. And yet not once in the twelve years that she lived there had she stopped to enjoy a sunset.

The sunlight streamed in through the glass doors. Well, it filtered in at any rate. Meredith noticed the glass was filthy. She walked back to the living room and reached to open the sliding door. It stuck. She tugged. It stayed stuck. She let it be.

She stood at the door and watched through the dirty windows as the sun set, turning the Pacific Ocean deep shades of greens and blues. As the last of the sun slid away, she faced the living room. She thought of the comfy sectional in Grace McDonald's basement. A smaller sectional would easily fit in her space and leave room for a coffee table and maybe an upholstered chair for reading. Add a picnic table and a grill on the deck, and she could have friends over. Therein lay the problem.

When Meredith stopped to think about it, which wasn't often, she realized she never had bothered to buy furniture to host a party because she never really had set down roots in Malibu. Sure, her business was flourishing, and she was financially sound. But she worked more than was good for her. Work had been her answer to everything since she had lost her parents. She had worked her way through college to keep her mind too busy to think about it. She had built Errands, Etc. by doing the jobs of three people. Working hard made everything better.

The only luxury she indulged in was to scour flea markets for vintage clothes. Her place may not have furniture, but the larger bedroom was stocked from floor to ceiling with designer jeans, pretty blouses, peasant-style dresses, and evening gowns cast off from movie studio sales—a collection worth a small fortune that she had collected in what little free time she allowed herself.

The first pangs of a headache beat at Meredith's temples, and she closed her eyes. That didn't help at all. Every time she shut her eyes, she saw Francis Ferguson lying dead on the floor. Then the image of her parents' bodies in the morgue followed. And the old gnawing pains started to work their way out of wherever they hid when she was strong enough to fight them down.

Meredith opened her eyes and told herself to stop with the pity party and get on with it. She was tired and hungry. She would feel better after a shower and something to eat. In the morning she would be rested and strong and ready to work. Because work would solve everything.

Or she could give herself a few hours off and scour the shops on La Brea. Maybe she could take David along as a way to make up for yelling at him.

She felt better immediately. Suddenly she had a plan, a goal, a way of taking charge of the situation before her emotions got the upper hand.

She jumped in the shower and did a quick change into clean jeans and a pretty cotton blouse. She pulled on a pair of cowboy boots so soft they felt like slippers. She found a leather jacket to complement the boots and transferred her wallet, gun, and cell phone into a great bag that pulled the whole outfit together.

She was in the mood for clam chowder, and she knew just where to find it. Right at the end of her driveway at a local joint called the Beach Shack.

Chapter Twenty

By the time Happy Hour rolled around, I was beat.

After taking Dot home, Grace hijacked me straight to my orthopedic appointment, thereby eliminating the nap I felt I needed more.

David was in the waiting room, working his phone, when Grace handed me over. The doc turned out to be a very busy woman wearing fabulous shoes. She was distracted, so I took advantage of that.

I lied and said I could wash my hair, no problem. I explained how vital it was to my job that I drive myself around. I promised that I understood that pain medication, alcohol, and driving do not mix.

Before you could say, "I have more interesting cases to see," the doc told me to use my discretion as to whether to wear the sling. She gave me written permission to drive and threw a new prescription at me as she swept out the door.

David used my newfound freedom as an excuse to lecture me all the way back to Malibu. Which he took his sweet time doing. I wasn't sure if he drove slowly to harangue me or because Stan's cop buddies stayed right on our tail.

"Darling, please, please think twice before you drive. I told Fred to bring you a nice little automatic-transmission something, but I don't know if he heard me…he was pretty upset about having to tow the Fury out of the mud."

"Oh, jeez. I need to call him and explain." I tried to lean down and pick up my bag, but a shooting pain in my shoulder set me back against my seat. Thank goodness David didn't notice.

"Poor Francis, poor, poor thing…if only she had stayed at Grace's house for one more night, we would just be cleaning up after a burglary instead of…"

A shiver raced through me. It suddenly hit me that I had driven Francis to her death. Literally. David glanced over at me and had the good sense to change his commentary.

But he continued to drive like a little old lady.

"Nurse Terry is settled into your guest room, darling, and she will stay there until you are healed."

"I don't think I need—"

"Really, Alana? You don't need her? Can you lift your arm over your head?"

"Yes!" I raised my left arm straight up, like I was asking for the teacher to call on me.

"Very funny, darling. Now try your right arm."

That didn't go as well. My right arm moved six inches from my side before I yelped in pain.

"Exactly. How are you going to dry your hair, darling?"

"I hardly need a nurse to—"

"Open this."

With one hand David pulled my new bottle of pain medication out of the pharmacy bag. It had the push-and-turn-to-open cap. I took the bottle in my left hand and tried to push with my right. The slight pressure on my right shoulder sent a flash of pain down my arm. I yelped again. Same thing when I switched the bottle to my right hand.

"You still need help, darling, so Terry stays."

"You could loosen the cap for me," I suggested, but I knew that argument was useless. Until I was healed enough to dry my hair while standing on my head, David and Jorjana were going to insist on Alana-sitters. I told myself to get over my stubborn independence and accept the help. Besides, given Stan's erratic work schedule, it would be soothing to have someone else in the house with me. The cops stationed on the curb were no help against the imaginary monsters hiding under my bed. Or in the corners of my mind.

David continued to lay out the plans for my evening.

David, Jorjana, Nurse Terry, Grace, and God knew who else had made arrangements for Stan to meet me for dinner at a local joint called the Beach Shack. Apparently the original idea of letting me go home to nap was abandoned. David worried aloud that it would be an hour or so before Stan was off work. He had to race back to Errands, Etc. and couldn't stay with me until Stan arrived.

That was fine with me. If I wasn't getting a nap, I intended to take some time sorting out the craziness of the last few days. Francis's death, my injuries, the secret Dot held for so many years. I needed some quiet time to think. And I prefer to think with a drink at hand. Painkillers be damned.

As we pulled into the parking lot of the Beach Shack, I told David I would be just fine by myself and not to worry. After all, the cops were still right on our heels.

"Well, yes, that is true, darling, but they will stay outside, and you will be alone inside and..." He glanced down at the bottle of pain meds.

"Is that what this is about? You're worried about me drinking and taking this medicine?" I shook the bottle with my good left hand.

"Stan said..."

"What did Stan say?"

I remembered waking up in bed and not remembering how I got there. Stan must have talked to Jorjana and David. The nerve of the guy. This irritated me to no end. I was guilty as charged but annoyed about being called on it.

"Now, darling, Stan said you may have accidentally had a bit too much wine last night, and you do have a concussion you know, and well..."

Oh, yeah, the concussion. I had forgotten about that, which explained why the wine had hit me so hard. If I know anything, it's how much I can drink before I should stop. And I also know how many drinks I can get away with when taking medication. But when you add a concussion to the recipe, well, then I'm out of my area of expertise.

"You're right, David," I said. I meant it. "I forgot I have a concussion. That's what the problem was last night, I'm sure."

"I'm so relieved to hear that, darling. When Jorjana heard that Stan had let you have wine, I thought she was going to...let's just say she was upset and leave it at that."

"I told Stan I was fine," I said in his defense. I felt it best not to mention the pain med I slipped in without Stan noticing.

David pulled up to the entrance of the Beach Shack and ran around the car to open my door. The cops parked strategically so they could see both the front door and the beach behind the building. I didn't know whether they were protecting me or making sure I couldn't escape.

David was on his phone as he opened the door to the bar for me. He was too engrossed in the conversation to say good-bye. I gathered business was booming at Errands, Etc., and Meredith couldn't possibly handle the onslaught by herself—like it would kill her to make a decision without consulting David first.

I waved to the cops and stepped inside.

The Beach Shack sits right on the sand in Paradise Cove. It's been there forever or at least before the tyrannical California Coastal Commission started laying down rules about where a building could go up. At any rate it houses a restaurant, an outdoor snack shop, and a bar. The bar is my favorite part. There is no view, poor lighting, and no tourists. And the barkeeps all know how to mix my favorite drink. What more could you ask for?

The place was busy, the regulars planted on barstools. Small round tables in the center of the room held candle holders covered in plastic netting. Red-vinyl booths lined the walls. One booth was empty, the one tucked away in the corner. I plopped myself down, nodded at the bartender, and prepared to settle in for a good think.

I like an old-fashioned bar. I like the cozy darkness. I like real linen napkins and heavy cocktail glasses that stay cold. I like music playing in the background that is loud enough to hear but not too loud to interrupt a conversation. Sometimes I like to sit on a barstool and listen to the nonsense that is discussed under the influence of alcohol. Other times I like to hide away in a corner and contemplate my own thoughts. I appreciate the protocol followed in the Beach Shack—no one will bother you if you bother no one. The rest of the world could learn a thing or two from that.

My Usual arrived promptly. I savored the first sip, and I kept my promise to David by not gulping down a pain pill. Not that I could get the bottle open. By my third sip, I was deep into the thoughts I wanted to think.

I had a lot to sort through. So much had happened within forty-eight hours.

Was that all the time that had passed since my lunch with Francis? How could a simple request go so wrong? If only I had backed Grace up and advised Francis to spend one more night at her daughter's house. Or if only

I had just taken Francis home to my house. Like David said, Francis would still be alive and her family dealing with a burglary instead of planning a funeral. The regrets that "if onlys" bring took me to the end of my drink. Not that the drink solved anything. Something about the robbery nagged at me. And it wasn't that the cops might think I'd had a hand in it. Something else just didn't add up. I couldn't figure out what exactly bothered me. I chalked it up to the concussion and signaled for another drink.

My second Usual led me to mull over the actions of my nearest and dearest. I had to remind myself that they all meant well, and I was lucky to have them. And if they were going overboard with their attentions, it was because they loved me and were concerned about my welfare. Which just reminded me of Stan's poorly timed declaration of love. Which I quickly put to the back of my mind then thought about less threatening developments.

I wasn't sure which intrigued me more, that Francis kept the secret of being George's mother or that Dot also kept the secret but never spent the money Milton sent to her. Or that Milton could produce baby George out of thin air and no one questioned him. Or that Francis could turn her back on Dot after all they had gone through together. Or any of it really. That generation sure knew how to button their lips about distasteful facts. Dot had said, "Things were different then." Were they ever. In today's world the whole story would be played out on the gossip websites and come and go before you could say, "illegitimate." I couldn't say what was worse, letting a secret fester for sixty years or displaying your dirty laundry in public. Seemed to me there should be some kind of civilized middle ground.

I don't know how long I thought my thoughts, but there were two empty glasses on the table when Meredith Mackenzie wandered into the bar.

Meredith wore jeans, a vintage blouse, and a nicer-than-average leather jacket. Her hair was down and fell in loose waves around her shoulders. She looked young and hip, and that annoyed me to no end. She carried a stunning leather handbag. I recognized the logo and was impressed. Business must have been damn good at Errands, Etc. No wonder David was so harried.

Meredith didn't look happy, though. She scanned the bar with a frown, and it didn't let up when she spotted me.

With nowhere to hide, I waved to beckon her to join me.

"Tough day?" I asked, as she slid into the booth.

"Yeah, we're swamped, and I took it out on David. I owe him an apology."

"Send him a text," I suggested. "He seemed a little frantic when he dropped me off. You know he'll just stew on it all night. You don't want to start tomorrow off with him in a tizzy."

"No kidding." Meredith deftly typed a message on her phone. "He does take things hard, doesn't he?"

She finished the text and dropped her phone back into her gorgeous bag.

"We moved back into our offices today too," she said with a relieved smile. "Thanks again for letting us barge in on you."

"My pleasure." I even sort of meant it. Then I remembered I had rent to pay. I waved the bartender over.

"What are you drinking?" I asked Meredith.

"I'll have a diet Coke with a slice of lime," she told the barkeep.

"I'll have another one of these," I said, and then to Meredith, "You sure you don't want anything stronger?"

"No, I don't drink," she said.

"Why?"

She looked at me in a manner that made me think she had answered this question before. "My parents were killed in a crash involving a drunk driver." She sounded very matter-of-fact about it, so I asked when it had happened. "Sixteen years ago. It was the day before I graduated from high school."

"Oh, I'm sorry. Do you have any brothers or sisters?"

"A brother." Her face clouded. "We're…estranged."

Not much to say to all that. I have an entire tree of family members I avoid.

The drinks arrived. Well, my drink and her diet Coke arrived.

"You're out of your sling," Meredith observed.

"Yep, just saw the doctor today, and I'm supposedly as good as new."

I wasn't, but nothing gets around faster than bad news. The last thing I needed was my nearest and dearest hearing I had complained about anything.

"Your jaw is still bruised, though." Meredith leaned over to get a good look at me. "Does it hurt?"

"A little," I admitted, then suddenly self-conscious I asked, "How bad does it look? I haven't looked in a mirror since this morning."

"I've got some stuff in my bag." Meredith pulled out a compact. "Lean over here, and let me see what I can do. It's the least I can do."

If you had told me I would ever let someone touch up my makeup in public, I would have seriously doubted your sanity. And if you had said I would let Meredith Mackenzie that close to me, I would have called you delusional. But there I was, turning my head so she could pat some coverage onto a bruise she herself inflicted.

"There, much better." Meredith closed the compact with a click. Just as George Ferguson entered the bar.

If Meredith had looked unhappy when she walked in, George looked like he wanted to put someone in a headlock and beat him to a bloody pulp. He stood at the threshold, his face a deep red, his arms slightly bent, as if preparing to start swinging. Right on his heels was a cheap-looking redhead who wrung the handles on her purse and looked like she would rather be facing a firing squad.

George nodded a curt greeting to one of the regulars at the bar. He made his way through the tables like the bad guy scouring the crowd for the sheriff. The happy chatter of the place dissipated as unease spread through the room. George was clearly displeased that all the tables were full. He turned to check out the booths. And then he spotted me.

"Uh-oh." I felt my stomach turn. "Do you have your gun with you?" I whispered to Meredith.

"Yeah, why?" Meredith followed my gaze. "Uh-oh."

I wouldn't say the bar cleared out like the Wild West films when the bad guy confronts the sheriff, but there was a definite change in atmosphere as George made his way to our corner booth. The redhead tottered after him like a nervous Chihuahua.

"You, you…" George stood at the booth and shook his finger at me. He then proceeded to spew out a long list of names for me, the least offensive being "nosy little bitch."

The bar fell silent.

"How dare you stick your nose into my business? That woman was *not* my mother!"

A more levelheaded person would have tried to calm him down. I, however, was three drinks into the evening and in no mood to play nice with anyone calling me names.

"As a matter of fact, Francis Ferguson *was* your mother, and I saw the birth certificate that proves it." Just for good measure, I said this loud enough for the whole bar to hear.

George's face turned from red to purple. His eyes all but bulged out of his head. He raised his arm.

I scooted toward the curve in the booth, as far away from George's reach as I could get. Out of the corner of my eye, I saw Meredith reach into her beautiful leather tote bag.

The redhead grabbed George's raised arm and tried to stop him. George responded by shoving his arm farther back—hard enough that she lost her grip and fell on her bony little behind. She let out a loud "whoo" as she dropped out of sight. To his credit, George turned around to see what happened to her.

And came face to face with Stan.

Stan wore a white button-down shirt, Levis, and a dark blazer. He had a bouquet of flowers in one hand. He looked like any regular guy about to meet his lady for a dinner date. But by the time Stan helped the redhead to her feet, he had put on his cop face.

"Let's step outside for a minute. OK, George?" Stan's voice didn't leave room for discussion. He placed the bouquet on the table by my drink. He reached out to take George by the left arm.

Meredith brought her hand back out of her bag, empty-handed.

Anyone with any sense would have realized it was time to cool down and walked out the door with Stan, but no one ever had accused George Ferguson of being sensible.

George jerked his arm away from Stan then followed through with a sharp right hook. His fist landed on Stan's cheek with enough force to knock Stan backward. Stan's eyes closed as his head whipped to the side. He kept his balance, though, and when his eyes opened, he made a move toward George. It was obvious Stan didn't intend to shake his hand.

Someone screamed. Others dashed out of the bar, drinks held aloft. I scooted to the edge of the booth, intending to nail George with a kick to his butt. But my injured arm hit the table, and a shooting pain stopped me cold.

George did not wait to see what Stan had in mind. He tackled Stan, and they both went down. Stan's head hit a table, sending drinks flying. Glasses shattered on the floor. A sharp smell of gin and vodka and beer filled the air. George landed on top of Stan and pinned his arms to the ground. I heard something go "snap," and Stan let out a painful cry that took my breath away.

George's legs straddled Stan, leaving a delicate region unprotected. Stan forcefully brought one knee up and walloped George in the nether regions. George hollered with the kind of pain that made the other men in the bar wince. Stan pushed George off him with one arm and jumped to his feet. He planted one foot on George's back while keeping his right arm close to his body. The arm was bent at a funny angle.

Stan still wore his cop face, although it was now streaked with blood streaming from a gash on his head. He kept his foot firmly planted on George's back as he assessed the situation.

"Are you OK?" he asked me. I nodded.

He looked over to the redhead who was cowering in another booth, her eyes as big and empty as balloons.

"Ma'am? Are you OK?"

She managed a nod too.

Then Stan caught sight of Meredith.

Meredith was on her feet with her gun in hand, just as my baby-sitter cops burst into the bar.

"Police! Put your hands up!"

I'll give the cops credit for not taking Meredith out. It did look bad. One guy on the floor; the other, a fellow cop, supporting his arm as blood streamed down his face while a tall brunette aimed a gun at them both. But the cops had the presence of mind to take stock before opening fire.

Meredith, to her credit, slowly put her hands in the air, the gun still in hand, and stepped away from Stan.

"We're OK," Stan said. "Just a little misunderstanding."

One of the cops planted a heavy boot on George's back as the other eyed Stan's arm.

"You need a medic, Stan?" He reached for the radio on his belt. "We can book this guy and hold him until you get checked out."

"No, don't book him," Stan said.

The cop who had his foot on George's back did not like that. "He assaulted an officer."

"It was a misunderstanding." Stan looked down at George, who was now moaning and trying to curl up in a fetal position. "I'm not in uniform. It was just a thing between two guys, OK?"

The cops exchanged a look; they didn't seem happy about it.

"Get him up," Stan said. The way he said it did not imply graciousness.

They liked that. Each one hooked an arm under George's armpits and yanked him to his feet. George wobbled and started to fall back down. The cops yanked him again, perhaps a bit harder. The redhead stayed in her booth, wringing the handles of her bag and not blinking.

"You can put your hands down, Meredith," Stan said. He pointed to her gun. "You have a permit for that, right?"

Meredith dropped the gun back in her bag. She produced a wallet and opened it to show Stan. He glanced at it then looked at Meredith with more admiration than I felt was necessary.

Stan turned back to George, whose color was returning to his face. "Are you done causing a ruckus, George?"

George glared at him, but it was from wounded pride. He managed a nod.

"Good. These officers are going to take you home, and then they're going to make sure your lady gets home safely. And you're going to pay for any damages to the bar, do you understand?"

George nodded.

The cops pushed George ahead of them and out the bar. The redhead tottered after them, her purse clutched to her chest.

I slid out of my booth and went to Stan's side. "You need stitches." I gently parted his hair to see the wound.

It was about two inches wide and pretty deep. The blood had soaked through his hair and was dripping onto his blazer.

"Ow." He winced as he let go of his right arm.

"And I think your arm is broken."

A bartender handed Stan a towel filled with ice. Another barkeep fashioned a sling out of a couple of linen napkins. Just another example of exemplary service from the Beach Shack.

"Can you drive us to the hospital?" I asked Meredith. I silently prayed the roads were open and we didn't have to return to Sosei.

"I'll bring my truck around," she said. "Just wait out front."

I tried to put my arm around Stan's waist as we followed her outside. But I tried with my right arm, and once again I yelped from the pain.

"We're quite the pair, aren't we?" Stan said, as the towel he held to his head turned red. "Are you sure you're OK?"

I assured him that I was fine.

"What the hell got into George Ferguson?" Stan asked me.

That explanation took us all the way to the emergency room.

Chapter Twenty-One

I awoke the next morning in my own bed. Outside the window the skies were blue. Inside the house I heard the distinct noise of someone rustling around in the kitchen doing something that smelled suspiciously of freshly brewed coffee and fried eggs. My suspicions were confirmed when Nurse Terry appeared at the foot of my bed bearing a mug of coffee.

"Good morning, Mrs. Fox! You slept very soundly last night. How are you feeling?"

She proceeded to help me sit up, fluff my pillows, and slip the sling back on my arm. I didn't protest the sling since she brought coffee to me.

"I'm feeling OK. How is Stan?"

"Mr. Sanchez was a little uncomfortable last night," Nurse Terry said. "He's awake now. I helped him clean up and dress, and he's eating breakfast downstairs. Would you like to join him?"

"Yes, please."

I let her help me pull on a robe and brush my teeth and told myself not to be so annoyed that she was able to help Stan and I wasn't. Between my sore shoulder and bruised jaw and Stan's broken arm and stitched head, we were lucky to have her help. Well, we were lucky that Jorjana sent her to help.

Stan sat at the breakfast bar, his arm in a bright new cast and a bandage covering most of his head. Bruises puddled under his eyes. But he was showered and shaved and dressed. And starving. He had no trouble shoveling scrambled eggs into his mouth using a spoon in his left hand.

"What does the other guy look like?" I said. I gave him an extra-long kiss just to show Nurse Terry I could do something for him that she couldn't. Yes, I know it was childish.

"I'm never gonna live this down," Stan said. "George Ferguson is a putz. I lost my footing. That's the only reason I went down."

I remembered the solid hit George landed on Stan, but for once I had the sense not to correct him. Stan's ego was as bruised as his eyes.

Meredith Mackenzie had lost no time in getting us to the hospital. It helped that my baby-sitting cops paved the way with sirens and lights flashing. Doctors and nurses swooped up Stan nearly the second Meredith came to a stop at the emergency room. Before you could say, "Cop down," he was medicated, x-rayed and stitched up, and his arm was set in a cast. Then the patrol cars escorted us to my house, where Nurse Terry settled Stan into my guest room and me into my own bed. It was fast and efficient.

And felt like a bad dream.

"Terry said you had trouble sleeping," I said.

I took the stool next to him at the bar. Magically a plate of scrambled eggs, a biscuit, and cut-up cantaloupe appeared before me. Along with blackberry jam, butter, and another mug of coffee. All stuff that was easy for me to get down with my sore jaw. I felt my annoyance at Nurse Terry ease.

"Yeah, my arm hurt like hell, and this cast is heavy. Every time I dozed off, I woke up. This is going to be a real pain in the butt. I can't drive. I—"

"No worries. I can drive you around," I said. "You'll just have to hang out here until you get the cast off."

It surprised me that I actually meant that. Me, who very recently had come unglued over his toothbrush hanging out in my bathroom. I wondered if the concussion was changing my personality.

"Mrs. Fox, I don't think you should be driving just yet," Nurse Terry said. "You took pain medication less than twelve hours ago. You and Mr. Sanchez must rest today."

"But I have an appointment," I argued.

"My kids have soccer games," Stan argued.

Nurse Terry looked at us like we had said we intended to spend the day doing push-ups.

"I have a meeting in Beverly Hills."

"My kids are playing in Thousand Oaks."

She shook her head.

She didn't know who she was dealing with.

"You can't keep us here," I said, truly believing it. "I made an appointment, and I'm going to keep it."

"I can keep you here. Mrs. York insists that you both rest. Besides, you don't have a car, Mrs. Fox."

"What? Fred was supposed to deliver—"

"He didn't." Nurse Terry looked a little too smug for my taste.

"Did Jorjana talk to him? Fred works for me and—"

"I need my kids to see that I'm going to be OK," Stan interrupted. "It's hard enough for them that their dad is a cop. I quit Homicide so I could have more time for them."

That softened her up.

"Perhaps I could call Mrs. York and ask her to send a driver over."

"Please do," I said. "And tell her I would like to talk..."

I didn't get to finish. Nurse Terry swept out of the kitchen and down the hall to the library. Likely to complain to Jorjana that I was being difficult—like Jorjana had never heard that before.

"Stan, I can drive. I'm fine."

"Let Jorjana help. Do you really want to fight the traffic all the way down to Beverly Hills today?"

He had a point. It would be nice to have someone else deal with the idiots on the road. Thinking about idiots on the road reminded me of the baby-sitters in the patrol cars. And the reason they were there.

"What's the latest on the investigation? Are there any leads on who broke into Francis's house?"

I couldn't bring myself to say the "m" word. I was still struggling with the fact Francis Ferguson was dead, much less murdered.

"Yeah, a couple of things have come up. You don't have any recollection of being hit?"

"No. Something hit me hard from behind, and I went out."

"If you had to guess, what do you think you were hit with?"

"I have no idea. It all happened so fast. What are you getting at?"

Stan glanced down the hall. Nurse Terry was on the landline at my desk, probably talking to Jorjana, judging from the tone of her voice.

"We never had this conversation," Stan said quietly. "Mark Ferguson walked through the house yesterday with the detectives. There doesn't appear to be anything missing. The safe was open, but all of Francis's jewelry was there, and apparently there was a lot of it."

"Maybe the burglar didn't have time to grab the jewelry."

"There was plenty of time," Stan said. "She had been dead a couple of hours by the time we got there. She was dead; you were unconscious. Whoever did this had time to pick the place clean. Assuming that's what they intended."

"What do you mean?"

Stan leaned closer to me.

"It bothers everyone on this case that a burglary was attempted the day of that storm. Every cop worth his badge knows that burglars stay home and wait out storms. Sure, after a flood or a fire, you can count on looting. But not in the middle of the disaster.

And particularly not in a place like the Fergusons' at the bottom of the canyon like that."

"Are you saying someone was waiting for Francis to get home?"

"I'm saying the investigators don't know what happened. But they're willing to bet it wasn't a burglar looking for jewelry. He wanted something else in that house, but no one can figure out what it was."

"I wish I could remember something, but I don't. Why did you ask if I knew what hit me?"

Stan glanced down the hall again. Nurse Terry was just finishing up her call.

"It's the weirdest thing. The coroner found strands of something under Francis's fingernails and in the cut on her face. It looks like her attacker was armed with a stalk of bamboo."

Believe me, I had no idea what to think of that.

Chapter Twenty-Two

Nurse Terry returned to say Mrs. York would arrange for cars for both Stan and me. She then fussed over us until we finished breakfast. Then she sent Stan back to bed to rest and helped me shower and dress properly for my day. By the time the driver showed up, I was ready to go anywhere with anyone. Just get me away from bossy Nurse Terry.

I was settled nicely into the back of the Bentley, the driver headed toward Beverly Hills, my cop sitters following at a reasonable distance, when my phone rang. It was Dot Derringer.

"Good morning, Dot."

"Hi, Alana! Listen, I was just chatting with Celeste Monte, and she said you was going down to see her today. Mind if I tag along?"

I hesitated before answering. Not that I minded bringing Dot along, especially since I wasn't driving. I was surprised to hear that she had talked with Celeste. For some reason I had assumed that none of Francis's friends had stayed in touch.

It appeared I was wrong. I hate to be wrong.

"Of course, Dot. We're just leaving my house now. Do you mind calling Celeste and telling her we'll be a bit late?"

"Sure thing. You coming with Grace again?"

"No, I've got a driver today."

"Miss Fancy Pants, huh? I'll polish the crown jewels then."

***

Dot's front door was opened by one of the women from the dining room. Dot's dog, LuLu, greeted me by running in circles and barking.

"Missus no ready," the woman said over the barking. "She say you come in."

I stepped inside. The woman scurried back to the dining room and took her place at a computer on the table. LuLu took her spot on her satin pillow on the loveseat. The little dog looked at me expectantly, as only a dog can. I took the hint, sat down next to her, and patted her head.

"That you, Alana?" Dot hollered from somewhere in the house.

"Yes, it's me," I hollered back. LuLu frowned as I stopped petting.

"Set down and make yourself comfortable. I'm almost ready!"

The women in the dining room kept at their work. Seemingly endless supplies of items were retrieved from around the house. There did appear to be some order to it. Tools and other hardware came from the direction of the garage. Beanie Babies and dolls were stored somewhere off the dining room. Old vinyl records were housed in bookshelves in the hallway. If I had to guess, I would have said that every room in Dot's home was devoted to the storage of all the stuff.

It was an odd way to live, no doubt about it. Not unlike living in a used-goods store, albeit a very busy used-goods store. I wondered where Dot slept. Or cooked. I got up and wandered toward the kitchen. The women at the table ignored me as I walked by with LuLu on my heels.

Dot's kitchen was a galley style that connected the dining room with the family room. There was no way the cookies she had served Grace and me were baked in there. The fronts were missing from the cabinets. Stored on the shelves and stacked on the counters was a collection of Fiesta ware dishware the likes of which I'd never seen. A riot of orange, red, gold, deep blue, green, and ivory dishware covered every flat surface in the room. There were dishes, bowls, vases, and candlesticks. There were salt and pepper shakers, ashtrays, and cups with saucers. Coffeepots, carafes, and casseroles. A veritable circus of ceramics.

I'm no expert, but I knew enough to know I was looking at good-quality stuff. The kind of stuff collectors lust after. There must have been tens of thousands of dollars of dishware stored in the kitchen.

LuLu trotted past me and made her way into the family room. There was no room for a family in there. Floor-to-ceiling shelving lined the walls, and three rows of shelving took up the middle of the room. Here lay boxes of dolls, storage boxes filled with Beanie Babies, and those plastic toys I've heard McDonald's gives out to kids along with saturated fat and salt. Again I estimated the collection to be worth a small fortune.

"Alana, where are ya?" Dot called out.

LuLu and I made our way back to the front room. Dot was dressed. I'm going to be kind here and say that Dot's outfit was inspired by her Fiesta ware.

"You have quite a collection," I said. "I've never seen anything like this."

Dot looked hard at me as if searching for criticism. Finding none (I was truthful; I never had seen anything like her house), she relaxed.

"You wanna see something? Come with me."

She headed down the hallway. LuLu very politely waited for me before following.

The walk down the hallway cleared up one question. Dot slept in a small bedroom in a full-size bed with a twin bunk above it. The rest of the room held her clothes, which were hung on rolling racks. The closet lacked a door and was stuffed with handbags and shoes. I deduced the room was Dot's, given the brilliance of the wardrobe. Two other rooms stored more of her collections: books, sets of crystal stemware, cowboy boots, board games.

At the end of the hallway was a door secured by four locks. Dot pulled a set of keys out of her handbag and carefully unlocked each one. As she pushed the door open, I noticed it was a heavy, fire-safe door, not a flimsy particleboard one like the others in the house.

LuLu planted her little butt just at the threshold.

"Lu's not allowed in here, and she knows it," Dot said. "You can come in, though."

I passed from the hallway into another world. The room stored the oddest of Dot's collections by far. Dome-topped wooden trunks, black satin capes, top hats, canes, stacks and stacks of books, copper kettles, stainless-steel pots, red ceramic cylinders, playing cards, dice. Along one wall shelving held heavy glass bottles. The room was packed from floor to ceiling. And the net effect was kind of creepy.

"My late husband was a magician," Dot explained. She picked up a small poster and handed it to me.

MYSTERIOUS! CHILLING! THRILLING!

SEE THE AMAZING FREDERIC

DERRINGER PERFORM

HIS FEATS OF MAGIC!

WITH HIS BEAUTIFUL ASSISTANT, DOT

There was a caricature of the Amazing Frederic holding a top hat and magic wand. In the background was a drawing of a curvaceous blonde showing a lot of leg. The show had played at four and nine o'clock during October 1949 in an obscure club in Las Vegas.

"Wow, Las Vegas. Very impressive." I handed the poster back to her. I didn't mention that the adjectives got bigger billing than she did.

"Yeah, well, it paid the bills," Dot said. She put the poster back in place like she was returning the Magna Carta to a hermetically sealed chest.

"Is this all of his…uh, stuff?"

"No. His things are in here." Dot opened one of the domed trunks. An aroma of sweat and mothballs floated out.

"Freddy specialized in sleight-of-hand tricks, so he didn't have a lot of props." She pulled a tray from the trunk. "See…coins, cards, a few shot glasses. Freddy's gift was how well he could tell a story. He got the audience distracted with jokes and won them over. It's all in getting the audience to fall in love with you, and then they'll believe anything you direct them to."

"Sounds like Freddy would have made a good politician," I said.

"He was a good man after all was said and done."

"Did he collect all this as a hobby?"

Dot put the tray back and closed the trunk solidly.

"Freddy didn't collect this—I did. This is gonna pay for my retirement once I sell it."

I looked around the room again. Given the state of the economy, Dot's collection was probably as solid as gold bouillon. Assuming she could find someone willing to pay for the stuff. Which seemed like a waste of time considering the nest egg she had in the bank.

"Why don't you retire on the money Milton Ferguson gave you?"

You would have thought I had asked Dot how much she weighed.

"That money is ill-gotten gains! I won't be beholden to Milton Ferguson, even if he is dead!"

"What are you going to do with it then?"

Dot's face hardened. "I don't know. I'll find a good use for it. Someday. I'm gonna pay for my own retirement with my own hard work. I can take care of myself."

Of that I had no doubt.

"How much do you think this is worth?" I had to ask just one more personal question. I'm nosy like that.

"To the right person, it's worth a bundle. The books are all out of print. There are tricks in there no one has seen in years. I'm working on finding a buyer, but I'm not gonna sell this to just anyone. I'm gonna sell this to a woman magician."

"Are there any women magicians?"

Now that she mentioned it, I couldn't think of any off the top of my head.

"Wouldn't someone like David Copperfield have the resources to buy this?"

For the third time in less than five minutes, I ticked Dot off. But this time I really pushed a button.

"There aren't very many women magicians because women have been shut out of magic! You know how many women are performing at the Magic Castle this week? One! In Vegas? None! If women had a chance, there would be plenty of 'em, believe you me! I'm not letting the likes of David Copperfield or any other *man* get hold of any of this!"

She swept her arms around, nearly decapitating me in the gesture.

"Whoa, Dot! I really hit a nerve there."

She was trembling.

A whimper sounded from the hallway. LuLu peeked around the corner, her little black eyes wide with concern.

"Lu, hush. It's OK," Dot said. She waddled over and picked up the little dog. LuLu tried desperately to calm Dot down with puppy kisses to her cheek. "Alana, I spent a lifetime watching from the sidelines, and it just gets to me how the men got all the breaks. My Freddy, he was a good, good man. He could tell a story and make you laugh 'til you peed your pants, but bless his soul, he wasn't that great of a magician. I taught him most of his act, and we did well enough. But I was the one with the talent. Given the chance I could have been really, really good. Times were different then. No one wanted to hire a woman magician."

"Why?"

"It goes way back to when a woman who practiced magic was considered a witch. You heard of the Salem witch trials?"

I had.

"So that label stuck. Men got to be the magicians, and women got to be the assistants. People accept that a man can perform magic, but they want the women to just stand around and be beautiful." Dot sighed. "Yeah, I could have been something. But I couldn't catch a break."

I had to wonder what had possessed her to collect all that magic paraphernalia if Freddy never used it. "Why do you have all of this stuff?" I asked.

"Well, now that's a whole 'nother story. Freddy wasn't a great magician, but he was a great gambler. I learned early on to take most of his winnings and invest in collectibles. That way he couldn't gamble away our savings. At one time or another, no one wanted Fiesta ware or Madame Alexander dolls or old cowboy boots. I got the magic props from pawnshops around Vegas. The other stuff I picked up here and there. We spent most of our time on the road, so everything had to be small enough to fit in the trunk of a car. That was a real shame 'cause I saw a lot of antiques that would leave me sitting pretty now."

"What about the Beanie Babies and the McDonald's toys?" I just had to ask. Being nosy again.

Dot sighed. "That was all Freddy. The gambler in him fell for that Beanie Baby crap. And the man had a hankerin' for Chicken McNuggets. Probably what killed him in the end. Enough of this. Let's go see Celeste."

"Speaking of Celeste," I said, "I thought you and the other ladies never saw each other after Francis had George. And now you tell me you just called Celeste. What's up with that?"

Dot smiled. "You never asked me if I kept in touch with Celeste. First rule of magic is to train the audience's attention where ya want it to go. I wanted to know what Frannie was up to, so I kept your attention on her."

"Well played, Dot," I said with a grudging admiration.

"And I'm not done yet. What did George say when he found out his real parents were Frannie and Milton?"

That story took us all the way to Beverly Hills.

Chapter Twenty-Three

The difference between Beverly Hills and Malibu has as much to do with attitude as it does location. In Beverly Hills one dresses in full dressage, fires up the Range Rover, and drives out of town to spend quality time with one's steed in a well-groomed and air-conditioned equidome. In Malibu you just throw a bridle on the horse grazing in the front paddock and explore the trails in your own backyard. My point is while there's plenty of money in both zip codes, the residents enjoy their cash in far different ways.

Celeste Monte enjoyed her cash in a time-honored Beverly Hills tradition. Her home lay above Sunset Boulevard, within spitting distance of the Beverly Hills Hotel. A gate at the street of course. The chauffeur buzzed, and the gate flew open. The cops scooted in on our tail. A long driveway ran past the tennis court. A small army of Mexican gardeners worked to restore the lawn to its prestorm perfection. The house itself was a two-story Mediterranean with a circular drive and a three-car garage.

I estimated the house to be in the six-mil range, average-ish for the neighborhood. The beautifully maintained grounds would cost two grand or so every month. This being Beverly Hills, there would be a pool. Add a pool guy to the payroll and three or four housekeepers, judging from the size of the place. I figured Celeste was paying out six grand a month just on maintenance. Someone had money.

"What does Celeste's husband do?" I asked Dot. I knew by this time to assume the husband made the money.

"Lawyer. He's dead, though."

The chauffeur parked close to the front door and unloaded Dot and LuLu. The dog had sprinted out of Dot's front door and flown into the Bentley with so much determination neither Dot nor I had the heart to send her back inside. She fully enjoyed sniffing every inch of the car on our way down to Beverly Hills.

A front porch ran the length of Celeste's home. The doorbell hung next to a set of stained-glass windows surrounding a solid-wood door. Not as expensive as Richard Lafferty's front door but pricey enough. The bell sounded a low tone that seemed to come from the bowels of the house.

Celeste Monte opened the door herself. The housekeeper must have been otherwise occupied.

Celeste was tall for a woman of her generation and had the posture of a ballerina. Her snow-white hair was cut short. She had diamonds the size of grapes on her ears, and an emerald the size of a plum hung from a gold chain around her neck. She wore an ivory silk top and black pants. She had seen the inside of a plastic surgeon's office at some point. She had made return trips too, perhaps one more time than was necessary. Her overall appearance was that of well-kept money.

"Hello, Dot." Celeste's voice was as deep as her doorbell. She looked past Dot to the Bentley and then to the cops. She looked back at Dot, then at me, then my sling. To her credit she chose to let us in. I'm not sure I would have done the same.

"You must be Alana Fox." In lieu of a handshake and in deference to my sling, she touched my arm. Dot got a big hug.

A grand entry displayed a brilliant crystal chandelier. A curved staircase led to the second floor. Just beyond the entry lay the living room, a decent-size space with bleached oak floors, white-linen furniture, and a white grand piano. A marble fireplace big enough to roast a pig in was the attention-getter in the room. Not because of the ample fireplace but because of the artwork above it. There hung a life-size oil painting of Celeste Monte.

The painting depicted a much, much younger Celeste dressed in a purple gown and standing next to the white piano. She wore ruby-and-emerald drop earrings and a matching necklace. Her right hand rested on the piano, and her left hand hung at her side with a bouquet of red roses in it. Her left ring finger was well displayed and bore a diamond ring slightly smaller than a Frisbee. The brilliant color of the piece in the otherwise all-white room was riveting.

"Celeste! You got the painting finished!" exclaimed Dot.

"Yes, it just arrived last week. Do you like it?"

"I remember that gown," Dot said. "You can still get into it?"

"I can get into it, but I can't zip it up," Celeste admitted. "My housekeeper had to use safety pins to attach the back of the dress to my Spanx every time I had a sitting. It was a sight!"

Dot made all the right comments about the painting while I glanced around the room. It was beautifully decorated; there was no doubt. I recognized the furniture from a popular LA. design firm. Drapes flanking French doors that led to the pool were made of a Scalamandre fabric from the most recent collection. Mirrored side tables had not so much as a speck of dust much less a personal photo. The room felt like an altar set up to worship Celeste. And everything in it was brand spanking new. I wondered how long Celeste's husband had been dead. She obviously was done mourning him.

Through the French doors, a blur of white fur raced inside. LuLu yelped and jumped out of Dot's arms. She tackled the other fur ball, and the two of them tumbled outside and disappeared.

"That's my Figgy," Celeste said. "She and LuLu are sisters. Did I tell you, Dot, that I got on the list for the next litter?"

And they were off. Off on one of those aggravating discussions pet owners have about their dogs. Not quite as mind numbing as parents discussing their children but close. I gathered that Dot and Celeste were well acquainted with a local Havanese breeder. While the women caught up, I stood to the side feeling like a bareback rider in an English country manor.

"Forgive me, Alana. Where are my manners?" Celeste eventually remembered I was there. "Let's have a seat, shall we?"

We took our seats, Dot and I side by side on a couch. Celeste sat in a chair that faced the fireplace.

A maid appeared, carrying a tray with lemonade and shortbread cookies. The tray was sterling silver, the drinking glasses solid crystal.

"Alana, I confess I was taken aback by your call. I haven't spoken with Frannie in years, decades really."

"I can't believe Frannie is gone," Dot said.

"Poor girl," Celeste said. "To die so violently...it's just awful."

Celeste crossed her legs and fussed with her top. She took her sweet time arranging the folds. When she finally looked up, she seemed as torn up about Francis's death as a politician is when an opponent falls in the ratings.

I reached into my bag and pulled out the envelope for Celeste.

"Francis asked me to find you and Dot and Pat Scott," I said. "She wrote letters to each of you. After she...died...her children asked me to fulfill her wishes. Here's the letter she wrote to you."

I stood up and gave it to her. She held the envelope with both hands in much the same way Dot had held hers.

As if the paper could speak.

But the look on Celeste's face indicated she was afraid of what the letter would say.

She pulled the letter out of the envelope. Just like Dot, her face registered a range of emotions. But when she was done, her eyes were hard.

"I need a moment. Please excuse me, ladies." Celeste rose. On her way out of the room, she handed the letter to Dot.

Nosy gal that I am, I scooted next to Dot to read over her shoulder.

Dearest Celeste,

So many years have passed. Not a day has gone by that I have not thought of you. I miss our long conversations. I miss giggling over the studio gossip. I miss your advice on how to dress and arrange my hair. But most of all, I miss you.

We were such dear friends, yet I betrayed you. Can you find it in your heart to forgive me? Please understand that I did not realize how dear Milton was to you. You had so many admirers that I thought he was just another of your beaus. I was head over heels in love before I knew it. And so was he. We were well suited for each other in the end. We were married more than fifty-five years, and I loved him with all my heart.

I lost Milton just over a year ago. I heard from Lloyd Evans that you lost your Jack about the same time. Please accept my condolences. I know how hard it is to lose a husband.

I have kept a secret all these years because I promised Milton I would. Now that he is gone, I am ready to correct all the deceits from the past.

Dot and I left so suddenly that day because I was pregnant with Milton's child. Dot took care of me until the baby was born. That child is the baby boy Milton adopted after Lydia's child was stillborn. I am George Ferguson's real mother. Now that Milton is gone, I am ready to tell George the truth. As I said, I want to put all the hurts to rest.

Celeste, I would like to reconcile with you if you will have me. It is my fondest wish that you and I and Dot and Pat spend that weekend at the Hotel del Coronado that we planned so long ago. Just the four of us, like old times! But this time the Tom Collinses are on me!

Alana Fox is delivering this letter for me because I am still a coward and am afraid to face you myself. Please let Alana know if you are willing to see me again despite everything.

With all my love,
Frannie

"Hmmph!" Dot was displeased. "Did Frannie really think I would run out on Celeste without tellin' her what I was up to?"

"I thought you said no one else knew about the baby except you and Milton and Francis?"

"Yeah, I said a lot of things," Dot said. "Yesterday I didn't know you from a hole in the wall, so I was still keeping Frannie's secrets."

I thought about this. And I wondered how many more secrets these ladies were keeping.

"Celeste doesn't seem as upset as you and I are," I said. "Do you think she's still upset about losing Milton to Francis? It's been over sixty years…"

"Yeah, I know." Dot sighed. "Celeste can hold a grudge with the best of them. I don't think she's as mad about losing Milton as she is about losing his backing. Milton promised to make her a star, but when Frannie and him started messing around, he turned his back on Celeste."

"So Celeste still blames Francis?"

"Frannie wanted Milton for herself more than anything. She got him in the end, and then she forgot about her friends. She could have asked Milton to open a few doors for Celeste and me. He had the power."

"It seems like a long time to hold a grudge," I said, like I was the patron saint of forgiveness.

"Celeste wanted to be a star as bad as Frannie wanted Milton. Frannie had to know that. She could have helped Celeste out. She should have. We weren't gonna say anything about the baby. She should have trusted her friends."

"So how many people knew about the baby?"

"Well, Frannie and Milton and me. I told Celeste. And Milton got Lloyd Evans to set up the adoption. Lloyd was a lawyer back then. And Lydia's pa knew too."

That took me aback. Lloyd Evans was in on the secret? So that made six people who knew Francis was George's mother. I found it amazing the secret never came out. That generation sure knew how to keep its mouth shut.

Celeste came back into the living room. Her eyes were red. She held a handkerchief in one hand. In the other arm was a photo album. She sat on the larger couch with the album on her knees. She waved Dot and me over.

"I have some old photos here," Celeste said, as Dot and I settled next to her. "I can't remember the last time we looked at these. Can you, Dot?"

Dot clearly was not happy to see the album. She looked at it as if it were a writhing snake.

The album cover was made of deep green leather with a large "C" engraved on it. As Celeste opened it, a musty smell arose. The pages were a thick paper and deeply yellowed. Black-and-white photos were held in place by little V-shaped metal corners. Under each photo someone had meticulously written captions with a fountain pen. The handwriting was an exquisite, very feminine scroll.

The first page held that photo of the four young women posing in front of the Hotel del Coronado. I saw it differently now that I had met three of the four. Francis stood in front of the others. She was petite, with her hair worn shoulder length and fashioned in soft waves. She smiled broadly at the camera. Behind her was Dot, a busty young woman with solid thighs and dark lipstick. Her hair was worn up and held there with a bandana. Her smile suggested she was ready for a good time. Next was Celeste, taller than the others and very slim. I suspected that at the time the photo was taken, Celeste hated her thin frame. Her hair was blonde, and her smile was wan. She seemed to lean away from Francis.

Pat Scott stood next to Celeste. Pat was the beauty in the group. She had the hourglass figure so envied in the forties. While the others were in skirted, one-piece suits, Pat wore a two-piece consisting of a halter-top and short shorts. She stood with one hand at her waist and her leg turned to a flattering angle. Pat wore her hair long and parted to the side. She had big eyes and a pretty mouth. She had the kind of good looks that the camera loves, and she appeared to know how to play to the lens.

"Look at Pat!" Dot cried. "She was a looker, wasn't she?"

"She certainly was," Celeste agreed. "I always thought she wasted her good looks working in the costume department. But then she couldn't act, could she?"

Celeste flipped through several pages before stopping. In the middle of the album were eight photos, carefully captioned. The shots were taken on a river, with four men fishing. I recognized a young Lloyd Evans and a young Milton Ferguson. The other two, according to the caption, were "Jack Monte" and "Mr. Attel." The date was May 5, 1946.

"*Mr.* Attel?" I asked Celeste.

"Yes, we were more formal then," she explained. "Lydia's father was much older than I, so I called him Mr. Attel. This was taken at the Attels' ranch outside Yosemite. Lloyd Evans invited me to go to this big house party the Attels held every year. It was a big social deal. Stupid girl that I was, I went just to be close to Milton."

Celeste turned the page. The next eight photos showed a spacious ranch house. Photos from inside the house were of the other houseguests.

"This is Lydia Attel." Celeste pointed to a young woman holding hands with Milton Ferguson. She was a gorgeous blonde with fair skin, a patrician nose, and wide-set eyes. Her eyes, however, had a haunted look, as if she were desperately trying to forget something awful. She was also pregnant.

"This is how Milton broke things off with me," Celeste said. "By getting Lloyd to bring me to the Attels' place and making me spend a long weekend with his pregnant wife. Nice guy, huh?"

"I told you and Frannie to stay away from Milton," Dot just had to say. "He was trouble from the word *go*. I told you."

"I see you started the discussion without me."

This came from the entryway. Celeste, Dot, and I turned to see a woman standing just inside the front door.

"Pat! You made it!" Celeste rose and hurried to give the woman a hug. Dot dragged herself out of the depths of the couch and waddled after Celeste. Being the great deducer I am, I figured out the woman was must be the elusive Pat Scott.

If Dot had let herself go and Celeste had gone a little too far, Pat Scott got the aging gracefully thing down just right. She still had her hourglass figure, undoubtedly helped by a really good bra. Her hair was red with streaks of silver, worn long and pulled back into a low ponytail. She wore a long cotton dress belted with a turquoise clasp, sandals on her feet, and a light wrap around her shoulders. Her jewelry was the kind of stuff one collects on world travels—rustic beads and battered silver. But her eyes were what caught my attention. Pat Scott had the biggest, bluest eyes I had ever seen. The kind of blue you usually only see in flowers.

"You must be Alana Fox! I haven't been avoiding you. I just got back into town and rushed over here as soon as Celeste told me you were coming over."

Pat left the embraces of her friends and shook my hand. Firm grip, and she looked me smack in the eye. Up close her eyes were magnetic. It was impossible to look away from her.

"You must think I'm terrible for not returning your calls," Pat said. "The truth is I was so taken aback that I called Celeste and Dot first. None of us ever expected to hear from Frannie again."

At that moment I knew Pat Scott was in on Francis's secret, too. That brought the number to seven. Who knew who else was in on all of this?

"I knew I would track you down eventually," I said, as I tried to keep everything straight. "I wish I had known you were coming. I would have brought the letter Francis wrote to you."

I shot a look over at Dot. She shrugged as she lowered herself back to the couch. "I told ya, I didn't know you from Adam."

"Let's back up here," I said, as we all settled into the living room. "I'm confused about who knew what and when. Can one of you explain just how many people knew about Milton's affairs and the adoption?"

Dot and Celeste exchanged a look. Pat didn't even pretend to be surprised.

Dot said to Celeste, "Go ahead. You tell her. Frannie and Milton and Lydia are all gone now. And George knows the truth about his real mother. The cat's out of the bag."

Celeste slowly closed the album and began. "I met Milton on the studio lot. He was married to Lydia, but the marriage was rocky at best. She was a nightmare. Today we would say that she was bipolar, but back then we called her 'flighty'…or worse. Anyway Milton was so handsome and charming that I let myself be drawn in. He promised to make me a star, and I wanted that so badly that I went against my better judgment and fell hard for him. Of course, to keep up appearances, I dated other fellows.

"Then Frannie came along, and Milton lost interest in me. I kept hoping against hope that he would follow up on his promises to me anyway. We were good together, he and I. We would have made great business partners.

"I wouldn't accept that he wouldn't at least work with me, and I became enough of a pest that Milton got worried. So he got Lloyd to drag me along to that awful weekend at the ranch. Milton took me aside and promised to find someone else who would take care of me but only if I left him alone.

"So then I went back to LA and found out that Frannie and Dot were gone. Dot wrote me a letter and told me all about Frannie's pregnancy. I was devastated. I quit my job at the studio, and then Jack started coming around. It didn't take me long to realize this was the guy that Milton intended to take care of me. Fortunately I had the good sense to fall in love with him. Smartest thing I ever did."

Celeste looked drained. She slumped in her chair and fussed with her top again. She glanced at the portrait of her young self with a melancholy that belied her last statement. Marrying Jack Monte may have been the smartest thing she ever did, but it hadn't made her happy.

The mood of the room definitely dampened. I'd had just about enough for one day, but I wanted to get the story straight, once and for all, before my head exploded.

"So all of you knew Francis was pregnant," I summed up. "And Lloyd helped organize the adoption after Lydia's baby was stillborn. Do I have this straight?"

Pat smiled a bitter smile. "Lydia's baby wasn't stillborn. She was having an affair with her gardener. Milton took one look at that baby and knew it wasn't his. He was furious. He sent it away to an orphanage."

Chapter Twenty-Four

"He *sent* the baby away? How could he do that?"

Celeste and Dot appeared surprised too. Finally someone else was taken aback. I had begun to feel like the village idiot.

"And stop calling the baby an *it*. Did Lydia have a boy or a girl?"

I'm no fan of children, but I do recognize them as people. This may have been the first time I had defended a baby, though.

"The baby was a boy," Pat said. "Lydia was under anesthesia when the baby was born, so she never even saw him. The last thing Milton wanted was for the world to know that his wife had cheated on him. And the last thing Mr. Attel wanted was a half-breed grandson. It was an easy deception to accomplish under the circumstances."

I glanced out the French windows at the lawn being tended to by Celeste's gardeners. I could see how the fair-skinned Lydia and a dark-skinned Mexican gardener would produce a baby that wasn't blond and blue eyed. "Half-breed" did seem a bit harsh, however.

"How do you know all this?" I asked Pat.

"I was a nursing student at the hospital. The attending nurse told me." She turned to the other two. "I never said anything because I didn't want that poor girl to get in trouble."

"What good would it have done to say anything?" Celeste said with a shrug. "What was done was done."

I didn't share Celeste's nonchalance.

"The hospital let him give away the baby without Lydia's consent?"

I couldn't get past this. I can let a lot of atrocities slide, but stealing just sits in my craw. It goes back to losing my Easy-Bake Oven when I was six. Or my husband when I was forty.

"I know it sounds shocking, Alana, but things were different in nineteen forty-six," Pat explained. "That child would have suffered enormously growing up. To be not only a child of adultery but of mixed race would have been impossible. The Attels never would have accepted him as one of their own. He was better off in the orphanage."

"Pat's right," Celeste said. "That poor kid didn't stand a chance. It was better that he was branded an orphan and raised with people who loved him. And when Lydia died, Frannie got to raise George anyway. Who was harmed?"

Their cavalier attitude irritated me. We weren't talking about sending puppies to the pound. I remembered Grace saying that George's issues lay in the fact that he never felt he fit in anywhere. And who knew what had happened to Lydia's baby boy?

"I can't believe the hospital allowed this to happen," I persisted. "How could they let Milton get rid of the baby? He wasn't even the father!"

Celeste and Dot exchanged a look. One of those looks adults share when a naïve child insists that "there is too" a way to revive the dead goldfish. They may have been as surprised as I was to learn the baby was born alive, but they weren't at all surprised to hear that Milton was able to ship the kid off.

"Alana, remember we are talking about the forties," Pat said. "The baby was an illegitimate mixed-race child of an unstable mother. The hospital deferred to the men in Lydia's life—her husband and her father. That's how things were done then."

"Let me get this straight," I said. "Lydia has an affair with the gardener at the same time Milton has an affair with Francis. Two babies are born. Milton realizes Lydia's baby isn't his child. So Milton, Mr. Attel, and the hospital lie to Lydia and tell her that her baby is stillborn. Lydia's baby gets sent to an orphanage, and Milton arranges to adopt his baby with Francis."

I paused. Something was amiss. Well, a lot of things were amiss, but at least one detail was way off.

"Milton is named as the father on George's birth certificate," I said. "How could Milton adopt his own child?"

"Lloyd Evans drew up the adoption arrangements, and Lord knows what kind of fancy deal he made,"

Dot said. "Lloyd told Frannie to destroy the original birth certificate, but she couldn't do it, so she asked me to hang on to it. So I did."

"Did Francis know Lydia's baby was still alive?" I asked.

"I don't think so," Dot said. "At least she didn't as long as I was with her. Who knows what Milton told her after they were married?"

"Milton never told her," said Celeste, who sounded quite certain. "Why would he? Lydia was dead, and the baby was long gone. Frannie thought Milton walked on water. He never would have told her otherwise."

Pat was seated next to me, and she took my hands in hers. A tactic I know well because I use it myself. People tend to keep their attention on you when you're tethered to them.

"I know this is a lot to take in," Pat said. "We've kept these secrets a long time. The three of us were loyal to Frannie, despite how she treated us."

Dot and Celeste nodded. Celeste's earrings grabbed a ray of sunshine and shot little dots of light on the ceiling.

I agreed that it was a lot to take in. Keeping track of who knew what—and when they knew it—was like herding cats while blindfolded. I was a long way from my original errand of delivering letters. What had seemed like a nifty idea to reconnect four friends had turned into a nasty stew of dark secrets and hidden agendas. Not to mention Francis's death. How much better would it all have been if I had taken her home with me that night? I would likely be healthy, happy, and listening to four women reminisce about old times.

Or would I? Francis brought me into this mess because she was afraid the ladies wouldn't see her. I had dismissed that idea because I'd gotten caught up in the fantasy of four good friends reuniting after a lifetime apart. But as it turned out, Dot and Celeste didn't have a lot of good memories from 1946.

"Let me ask you something," I said to all three of them. "If Francis were still alive, would you have agreed to see her?"

"No," Celeste said, and there was no question she meant it.

"Probably not," Dot said.

"I don't know," Pat said.

The other two looked at Pat in surprise.

"I didn't have as much at stake in all this," Pat explained. "I was out of the group and in nursing school before Frannie got pregnant. But I knew what had happened, and I always felt a little sorry for her. She carried the burden of that secret for a long time."

"You felt sorry for her? Are you nuts?" asked Dot. "Frannie got everything she wanted in the end. She got Milton, and she got to raise George as her own. And then she had two more kids and lived like Her Royal Highness. Feel sorry for her? My foot!"

"She did get everything," Celeste said. "She got the husband, the children, and the life she wanted. And she did it at our expense while we kept our mouths shut all these years. If she had shown up on my doorstep, I would have called the police."

***

I left shortly thereafter. The discussion around the room heated up, and I didn't have the energy to deal with it. My shoulder ached, my head ached, and my heart was heavy. I made arrangements to meet with Pat at her home the next day. She agreed to take Dot and LuLu home. I found my way out of the house and into the Bentley. I told the driver to take me home. I was so beat that when we pulled out of Celeste's circular drive, I didn't notice the cops were gone.

The drive back to Malibu was just long enough for me to think. I had innocently agreed to deliver the letters to Francis's old friends. In exchange I expected to gather connections to start up a seniors' social club. What I ended up with was a dislocated shoulder, a concussion, a ruined car, an interrogation by the police, and a nasty secret that would haunt me forever. Stan had a broken arm and a bruised ego and had to explain to his kids that their dad was just fine and not to worry.

And then there was Francis.

My shoulder and Stan's arm would heal, but Francis was dead for good.

With a sigh I dug out my cell phone and started dialing. Once I delivered the letter to Pat Scott, I would fulfill my promise to Francis. Enough time had been lost in this whole ordeal. I needed to get my life back on track.

First call went to Jorjana. I got her social secretary on the line. He said Mrs. York was resting and asked if I wished to disturb her. I did not.

Second call went to Stan.

"Hey, gorgeous! Where are you?" He sounded upbeat.

"On my way home from Beverly Hills. Where are you?"

"On my way to the soccer game. Jorjana sent one of her guys in a Jeep!"

"You sound surprised by that."

"Yeah, I was worried she'd send a limo, which would be hard to explain to my kids."

I suspected his kids were the least of his problems. His ex-wife isn't a fan of mine. My sources keep me informed on her rants about "that snotty bitch on the beach." If Stan arrived at the soccer game in a chauffeured limousine, who knew what wrath she would lay on him.

None of that was my business of course, so I changed the subject. "When will you be home?" I asked.

"You mean back at your house?"

After a day of one surprise on top of another, I didn't expect to face yet another one. But sure enough, there one was. I had just asked Stan when he would be home, and I meant "home" not "my house." Toothbrush be damned.

"Yes. When will you be home?"

"That's the nicest question I've had all day," Stan said. "I promised the kids I would take them out for teriyaki after their games. I'll be back...I'll be *home* by nine. Will you wait up for me?"

I agreed I would.

"Hey, Alana, one other thing," Stan said. "Be careful until I get there, OK?"

"What do you mean?"

"There isn't a patrol car on you anymore. Since I'm recuperating at your place, my captain figured that was enough police protection. Didn't you notice they were gone?"

I turned to look out the back window of the Bentley. Nothing but the usual trail of Land Rovers, Priuses, and Mercedes.

"They're gone all right," I said. I told him to wish his kids good luck for me. He said he would. He wouldn't of course, but I was fine with that. We both said we looked forward to seeing each other. He said he loved me. I hung up.

I turned around to look out the window again. There were definitely no cops tagging along. I sat back. With Stan out for the day, Nurse Terry could lavish her full attention on me. Which made the odds of mixing up "the Usual" pretty slim. The evening ahead looked bleak. I needed some companionship, and I knew just where to get it.

I told the driver to set his sights on the Malibu Town Center.

Chapter Twenty-Five

The parking lot at the Town Center was dry, but sandbags still lined the walks outside the stores. All businesses were open. Beans had its usual line of customers out the door.

I thanked the driver for his service and sent him home. I climbed the stairs to the second-floor landing. I was in search of companionship. With Jorjana resting and Stan playing daddy, David Currie was the logical choice.

I opened the door to Errands, Etc. and found him standing on a stool directing the staff like a symphony conductor.

"Terry, load those baskets in the van when you are done. Jenny, give Terry a hand, and then grab the keys from Meredith and you deliver them...here are the directions. Peggy, when you finish addressing that stack of cards, wrap the presents Mrs. Thompson asked us to buy, and remember they are the birthday gifts, not the Hanukkah gifts. Everyone else help Todd and Phil sort through the boxes of lights! Let's move, people!"

On the wall behind David hung the whiteboard that is Errands, Etc.'s lifeline. Every day for the next week was jam-packed with pickups, drop-offs, wrapping, addressing, and decorating around Malibu. No wonder Meredith Mackenzie could afford such dandy handbags.

"Alana, darling! How are you? I am crazy busy just now—can I meet you in your office in a few minutes? I can't wait to show you what I've done, and the furniture is all to be delivered tomorrow! I *love* retail!"

It took me a second to follow his train of thought. It seemed a lifetime ago that David had carried me across the threshold of my new office and started planning a decorating scheme. The original plan was to throw up some paint, move in some furniture, and be done by Friday.

It was now Friday. And David, despite all that happened, had a retail delivery scheduled? The man was a wizard.

I blew him a kiss and walked next door. I found the key at the bottom of my bag and managed to let myself in using my left hand. I switched on the light.

The surprises that day just never ended.

The ugly fluorescent lights were gone. In their place were recessed lights that sent a soft glow through the reception area. The floor was covered in plush gray carpet. The walls were painted ivory. The plywood door that led to the back office had been replaced with an etched-glass door decorated with swirls and curls and sported an old-fashioned crystal knob. The place felt fresh and new and full of promise. I loved it.

I walked into the back office and dropped my bag on the floor. I stood where I suspected my desk would go.

David was big on placing furniture at an angle and likely would situate the desk so that it faced the center of the room. I could see out the window to PCH. To the left of the window hung a mirror that reflected the etched-glass door. It was a brilliant idea. I would be able to sit at my desk and see who was coming in the front door. This was going to work beautifully.

I entertained myself for a while by imagining the clients who would walk through the door, the parties I would plan at my desk, and the money I would rake in. It was a fun game for a while. But I got tired of standing around and wondered when David intended to show up. Then my shoulder started to hurt again, and I thought about why I was tired. Which led me to remember the convoluted conversations I'd had with Celeste, Dot, and Pat. And then I got to thinking about Lloyd Evans.

It seemed Lloyd's nose was in every corner of the story. From arranging adoptions to introducing a bothersome Celeste to her future husband, Lloyd had been Milton's go-to guy. My opinion of Lloyd had changed completely since the day I'd signed the lease. I once considered him an honest businessman with a big heart. Turned out he was anything but honest. The ladies may have thought it was OK to ship Lydia's baby away, but I sure as hell didn't.

I couldn't let the fate of Lydia's baby go. I decided to give Lloyd Evans a piece of my mind.

***

The receptionist at Lloyd's front desk was not his granddaughter, but she was tall and blonde. She took one look at my face and called Lloyd faster than you can say, "You don't pay me enough to handle this."

"Mr. Evans will be delighted to see you, Mrs. Fox."

We would see about that. But I conjured up a smile, and she let me through unattended.

Lloyd slowly got up from his desk to greet me. He looked tired. He looked about one hundred years old. I didn't feel the least bit sorry for him.

I bypassed the niceties and opened with, "You and Milton Ferguson were quite the pair. You want to explain yourself?"

That took him by surprise. He started then turned to look at the fishing photos on the bookshelf. I noticed one of the shots was from that fateful weekend at the Attels' ranch. Lloyd recovered of course; a lifetime of keeping secrets will give you that skill.

He sat back at his desk and indicated I sit as well. Normally I would have remained standing to preserve the advantage of height, but my shoulder convinced me to sit. So I did and waited for him to spin his tale.

"Alana, this has been a horrible week for us all. Tell me what is on your mind."

I told him. From the visit to the bank with Dot, to George's tantrum at the Beach Shack, to the trip down memory lane in Celeste's album, I brought him up to speed all right. Like he didn't know the whole story already. I will say he seemed a little shocked that Pat knew the baby was born alive.

"I worried that giving Francis those women's addresses would end badly," he said. "I feared they would have nothing to do with her."

That cleared up the question of how Francis knew how to contact her old friends.

"How could you agree to let Milton send that baby away?" I asked, not nicely either.

"That was not my doing," Lloyd protested. "Milton sent the child away before I came into the picture."

"Where did the baby go?"

"There was a convent in the Central Valley—Fresno, I think. They specialized in taking in children like that."

"Then you arranged for Milton to adopt his own child?" I said.

"There was no legal adoption," Lloyd said. "Francis relinquished custody of George to Milton. I did draw up some legal-looking documents for Milton to produce if anyone asked. No one did. Things were—"

"Things were different then," I said. "So I've heard. This whole story makes me sick. You and Milton were playing God. How dare you?"

"Now just a minute, Alana!" Lloyd held up his hand, as if that would stop my poor opinion of him. "Douglas Attel and Milton were playing God, if you must. But keep in mind that Lydia was mentally ill. I know it seems cruel, but Milton was doing what he thought best."

"Best for him," I pointed out.

"And best for Lydia. If it became known that she had an affair, she would have been ostracized. It would have been a huge scandal, more than she could have handled. Milton was not as cruel as you make him out to be. It was best for everyone for Lydia's baby to be given away."

I still didn't agree. But I didn't have time to argue further. David burst into the room, as pale as the white-linen furniture in Celeste Monte's living room.

"George Ferguson is in the hospital. Somebody broke into his house and beat him up. They don't think he will make it."

Chapter Twenty-Six

We made it to the hospital in record time.

The waiting room was crowded: Grace McDonald, Mark Ferguson, spouses and children, the cheap-looking redhead, and a couple of cops. Lloyd, David, and I barely squeezed in.

Grace and Mark looked shell-shocked. They huddled together on a couch, yet again holding each other up. Grace's husband spoke quietly into a cell phone in the corner. Mark's wife handed cups of tea around. The kids, assorted ages and attitudes, slumped around a table. The cops spoke with the redhead.

"He was so upset last night, I just couldn't stand him," the redhead said. "The cops dropped him off at his house, and I told them to take me straight home."

"What time did you return to Mr. Ferguson's home?" one of the cops asked.

"I called him this morning, and when he didn't answer, I got pissed off and went over there. I thought he wasn't picking up on purpose, and I was going to tell him off in person. That's when I found him."

"What time was this, Ms. Silver?" the cop repeated with an admirable patience.

"Time?" Ms. Silver was not quick on the uptake.

"Yes. What time did you discover Mr. Ferguson?"

"This morning, after he didn't answer his phone. I told you this…"

I couldn't listen to it anymore. I moved on to Grace.

"Grace, I am so sorry." I sat next to her on the sofa. "How is he? How are you?"

"He's out of surgery. They had to induce a coma. He was beaten badly." Her voice held no inflection. She sounded like a robotic recording.

"If he makes it through the next twelve hours, he has a chance," said Mark, who put the emphasis on "if."

"Excuse me. Can we have a word with Mrs. McDonald?"

The cops had given up on Ms. Silver, who stood alone, looking like an abandoned doll.

As Grace rose, David slipped in next to Mark and put his arm around him.

Lloyd moved to Ms. Silver's side. I joined him.

"Ms. Silver? I am Lloyd Evans, a family friend. I am also an attorney, if you have need to speak in confidence about any of this."

Ms. Silver was closer to fifty than forty, but she dressed like she was seventeen. Long layers of dyed red tresses, ample boobs squeezed into a tank top, and skin-tight jeans. Too much makeup, too bright lipstick, and a fake Vuitton bag completed the ensemble. But her eyes, underneath heavy lashes and thick liner, were sad. Truly sad. Ms. Silver was honestly fond of George Ferguson.

"I know who you are," she said to both Lloyd and me. "I'm Kaytee Silver."

"This must be a shock," Lloyd said in his very best trust-me-I'm-a-lawyer voice. "Can you tell us what happened?"

She could and she did.

It was pretty much what I'd heard her tell the cops. George was upset by the news that Francis was his mother. They went to the Beach Shack to have a drink, where he confronted me then fought with Stan. The cops dropped her off after delivering George to his house. She couldn't reach him by phone in the morning, and then she found him beaten and unconscious. Lloyd managed to get a time out of her—shortly before eleven.

"Do you have any idea who would do this to George?" Lloyd asked.

"No."

"Has he seemed upset by anything lately?" Lloyd persisted. "I mean, before he found out that Francis was his mother?"

That gave her pause. Of course, asking if George Ferguson was angry about something was sort of like asking if the sun rose every morning. The man was a walking lit fuse.

"He's been spending a lot of time in some creepy chat rooms lately," Kaytee said. "He has this crazy idea that his other mom isn't dead."

Lloyd raised an eyebrow, the lawyer equivalent of gasping out loud.

"Whatever made him think that?" Lloyd asked.

"He couldn't locate her death certificate anywhere," Kaytee said. "He's been obsessed with it. He checked records in every single state for the last sixty years. I told him to knock it off because he was getting some really weird messages from the creeps who hang out on those sites. You know, the kind of people who see a conspiracy in everything."

"Yes, that can be very disturbing," Lloyd answered. "Did George ever agree to meet with any of these people?'

"I don't know. I sure hope not." Kaytee's heavily fringed eyes grew wide. "Do you think one of them beat him up?"

"That I do not know. Have you told any of this to the police?"

Kaytee shook her head. Lloyd took her by the arm and led her over to the cops. He stayed by her side while they questioned her. I wondered whether Lloyd charged as much per hour as Richard Lafferty.

David left Mark and joined me.

"Darling, this is just awful," David whispered in my ear. "Mark just told me George was beaten with some kind of bamboo sword. George had hold of the thing when the ambulance arrived. Look, here's what it looks like."

David held a photo of a sword lying on a floor. It looked to be about a yard long and was composed of bamboo switches held together with straps. The handle was wrapped in duct tape.

"Bamboo?" A nauseating rush of adrenaline made me weak in the knees.

"Good heavens, darling! Did you see a ghost?"

"Stan told me there were strands of bamboo under Francis's fingernails and in the cut on her face."

David gasped. Now he looked like he had seen a ghost. "Alana, is this what you were attacked with?"

I had no idea but the sword looked fully capable of knocking someone out. Or killing them.

I felt the lump on my head and winced.

"Mrs. Fox, may we have a word with you?"

Apparently the cops were done with Kaytee.

I took my hand from my head and located my cell phone.

I hit number three on the speed dial.

Chapter Twenty-Seven

MEREDITH

Meredith Mackenzie stood in front of the whiteboard and stared at the errands. By her calculations, if she doubled her staff, found six more hours in every day, and added two more weeks onto the month, Errands, Etc. would be able to meet all its obligations. No worries, mate.

Friday afternoons were always hectic, but this Friday was more frantic than usual. Part of it was due to catching up after the storm. Most of it was due to an unexpected surge in business. Meredith headed back to her office, intent on contacting Pepperdine students in need of some quick cash. With a few extra hands, maybe it would all get done.

She had just sat down at her desk when she heard the front door open.

Now what? she thought, as she walked back into the workroom to see who was there.

Two cops stood by the door. They weren't in uniform, but they were cops. Meredith would have known this even without the badges they held out for her inspection.

It was not a social call. Meredith barely had time to identify herself as the owner of Errands.

"Do you know this woman?" One of the cops held up a mug shot of a young Asian woman.

Meredith felt her stomach churn.

"That's Jenny Shu. She's one of my employees. What's this about?"

"We'd like to question her. Is she here?"

Typical cop, not answering her question.

"No, but she should be back soon. Can't you tell me what's going on?"

"Can we look around?"

They weren't asking for permission. The cops swept past Meredith and into the back offices. Just then the front door opened, and in walked David with Lloyd Evans in tow.

"David, two cops are here looking for Jenny!"

David stopped in his tracks. Speechless.

Lloyd Evans stepped forward. "What do they want, Meredith?"

"They won't tell me. They're in the..."

The cops reappeared. One of them had a file folder in his hand. Meredith recognized it as one of her employee records. He opened it and read out loud. "Jenny Shu, age twenty-nine. Most recent address listed as Fresno. Who hired this woman?"

"I did," David said.

"Just a minute." Lloyd stepped forward. "I am Lloyd Evans. I am Ms. Mackenzie and Mr. Currie's attorney. Will you please show me some identification then tell me how we can help?"

The cops stiffened at the mention of "attorney." But they showed Lloyd the mug shot and produced badges. Lloyd made a show out of taking each one and writing down the badge numbers in a small notepad. Meredith wondered how much Lloyd was going to charge her for this unexpected legal service.

"Why are you interested in Jenny Shu?" Lloyd asked.

"Her legal name is Kiwako Ito. She has warrants out for her arrest in Fresno for burglary and assault. Her fingerprints were found on a weapon that was used in an assault today in Malibu."

"George Ferguson!" David cried out. Lloyd put a hand on David's arm, holding him back.

"Yes, sir," the cop said. "Do you know him?"

"We were just at the hospital with his family," Lloyd said. "How did you make the connection between Jenny Shu and Kiwako Ito?"

"When we ran her fingerprints through the system, we saw a search from an insurance company. We contacted the insurance company, and they confirmed that Errands, Etc. had hired her as 'Jenny Shu.'"

David looked like he would faint.

"Are you sure you have the right woman?" Meredith asked, even as she stared at the mug shot Lloyd held.

"Yes, ma'am. Kiwako Ito broke into the administrative offices of the Archdiocese of Fresno and assaulted a security officer. She used a bamboo sword called a…" He looked at his phone. "It's called a *shinai*. She was arrested but released on bail. She has a sick child, and her attorney pleaded for leniency."

The cop shot a dirty look at Lloyd.

Lloyd stood as still as a stone statue, his jaw clenched. "Why did she break into the offices of the Archdiocese?" he asked.

"No idea, sir, but she tore apart a records room in the basement of the building. The security guard saw her running away and tried to stop her. She beat the guy senseless with this *shinai* thing. It was all caught on a security camera."

"Does she have any priors?" Lloyd asked.

Meredith wondered where he was heading with this questioning.

"Yes, sir." The cop checked his phone again. "Seems she came unglued when her kid got sick. The kid needs some kind of transplant, and she took issue with the hospital. She threatened a nurse."

There was more, and it pained Meredith to hear it. Jenny's family had posted the bail for her release, but then she disappeared. She missed her court date, and then the family filed a missing persons report. The child was gravely ill. There was a husband and another child. It went on and on. No wonder the insurance company had taken so long to get back to David; Jenny's name didn't match her fingerprints.

The question no one could answer was why Jenny would abandon her sick child and her family and show up in Malibu to work for Errands, Etc. And why had she attacked George Ferguson?

The cops asked again. "Where is Kiwako Ito?"

Meredith glanced at the whiteboard.

"She's delivering baskets on Broad Beach. She should be…"

The cops swept out the door.

"Meredith, that girl accessed my most personal computer files," Lloyd said.

Like she didn't know. Meredith faced Lloyd head on and took the blame. "Lloyd, call a forensic computer specialist right away. I'll pay for it of course."

Lloyd turned on his heel and was gone

Meredith turned to David, fully intending to read him the riot act.

David was looking at his cell phone. He let out a small cry.

"George Ferguson just died."

Chapter Twenty-Eight

"Don't give me that look, Richard. You told me to call you before I talked to the cops."

Richard Lafferty grumbled something under his breath as he eased his Aston Martin into traffic.

I could have handled the questions from the cops just fine on my own. But for once, I did as told and called Richard before making a statement. It wasn't my fault he took his sweet time getting to the hospital. In fact he took so much sweet time that David and Lloyd Evans left. So Richard had to drive me home through some of Southern California's worst traffic.

"I'm not irritated with you, Alana," Richard growled. "I'm irritated at those nitwits that call themselves cops. Obviously a madman is targeting the Ferguson family. The cops should be getting fingerprints off that sword and catch this guy before anyone else gets hurt."

The sword was the subject of most of the cops' questions. I knew it was just a matter of time before it was identified as the murder weapon in Francis's death.

The cops were greatly interested in knowing how much of my free time I spent learning the martial arts. The answer to that was exactly no time at all. Then they asked if there was any chance my fingerprints would show up on the handle. The answer to that question was no. I then reminded them that I had been whacked in the back of the head and suggested that strands of my hair were likely stuck in the bamboo shaft. That was the point where Richard ended the discussion.

"Who would do this?" I asked Richard. "First Francis and now George. I can't make sense of it."

"There's something going on that we have no idea about," he said. "I could see that George would have enemies, but Francis was a sweetheart. No one had anything against her."

I thought back to Celeste's claim that she never would have welcomed Francis back in her life.

"There are always three sides to every story," I said.

"I guess we'll have to wait for George to wake up to find out which side is the truth," Richard said.

That was the end of that conversation. I spent the rest of the ride home listening to Richard bark orders into an earpiece that was somehow connected to his cell phone. It's a technology I don't understand, as all my cars have manual roll-down windows. But it gave me time to realize that I was tired right down to my bones. Which made me aware of a thumping ache in my shoulder. I was never so glad to see my driveway.

Richard dropped me off with a cursory wave. Cradling my arm, I made my way down the steps to the front courtyard. My shoulder hurt so much that even the sling didn't provide enough support. I needed pain-killers, a drink, and a nap. And I needed them now.

I heard a beep from my cell phone from the depths of my handbag. I chose to ignore it. I was done for the day.

My house was brightly lit up and smelled yummy as I stepped inside. Which reminded me that I wasn't alone. I found Nurse Terry in my kitchen, stirring a pot of something. In the oven I spotted biscuits baking. Outside, my back deck was still gone. None of this did anything to improve my mood.

"Good afternoon, Mrs. Fox," Nurse Terry said. "You look tired."

Afternoon? I felt like it was midnight. The clock on the oven read four forty-five. Damn. Not even late enough for a drink.

"I'm reheating this pot of stew and some biscuits I found in the fridge," Nurse Terry said. "When was the last time you took a pain-killer?"

I couldn't remember.

"How bad is your pain on a scale of one to ten?"

Truly I was more tired than anything. I confessed to level two in hopes that I could finagle a drink out of her.

No such doing. She poured out a couple of Tylenol and made a mug of herbal tea to go with it.

"Dinner will be ready shortly. Why don't you sit down and enjoy your tea while I get things ready?"

"Fine." I gave in. "I'm starving, though. Can I have a couple of those biscuits?"

I could. She pulled two out of the oven, slathered them in butter, and placed them on a plate. Then she looked at the mug, the plate, and my sling.

"Where would you like to eat this?"

"The library, please."

I followed her down the hall. Terry organized the tea and biscuits on the desk. I thanked her as I settled into my chair. My handbag went on the floor.

I waited until I was certain she had returned to the kitchen. Then, from a deep drawer, I pulled out a bottle of brandy and added a dollop to the tea. A couple of sips later, I felt a whole lot better about everything.

The biscuits were hot and filling. My library was quiet and cozy. By the time the Tylenol kicked in, the biscuits were gone and the teacup empty. I felt heaps better. In fact I felt well enough to get some work done.

There were just under a million messages on my house phone. I listened to two.

From Jorjana: "Franklin and I are dining in Santa Monica this evening. I do not wish to disturb your rest. Please ring in the morning."

From Fred: "I left the forty-one Caddie. It should be easy to drive one-handed."

Nothing from Stan. Not that I expected there to be. He gives his kids 110 percent of his attention when he's with them. And I wasn't going to interrupt that time with bad news that he could do nothing about. I do have a heart.

So all was well. Jorjana was entertained for the evening, and Fred had delivered a car. My work was done.

Then the house phone rang. It was Pat Scott.

"Alana, would you like to swing by and have a glass of wine with me?" she asked. "I'm home now, and I have to admit I'm really curious about the letter Frannie wrote to me. We could have a little Happy Hour, just the two of us."

What the hell. Stan would be gone for hours, and I felt a lot better after food and drink.

I told her I would be right over.

***

My 1941 Cadillac convertible coupe is a sweet car. Black exterior, black interior with maroon piping. I tossed my handbag on the seat and climbed in. Putting the key in the ignition sent shocks of pain through my shoulder. I managed to turn the key and start the car, but then I was faced with engaging the transmission. There was no way my right arm would lift high enough to reach the shift lever on the steering column. So, in an inspired maneuver that would give Fred a nightmare if he knew, I slid over to the passenger side and put the car in gear with my left hand. Then I slid back, backed out of the garage, and repeated the trick to shift into drive.

Fred was right. The Caddy was easy to drive with one hand.

I made my way to PCH and joined the traffic mess that's known as the Friday-evening commute. If that weren't annoying enough, the constant little beep from my cell phone turned into a ring. I knew from the ringtone that it was David, but I had no way of answering the call. I thought of Richard barking into his earpiece.

At times like that, I do yearn for the conveniences found in modern cars.

Pat Scott lived in one of Malibu's most unique neighborhoods, a mobile-home park called Paradise Cove. Don't let the term "mobile home" fool you. These are million-dollar abodes with endless views of the Pacific Ocean. I pulled up right in front of Pat's place, set the brake, and dug my phone out of my bag. David had called three times since I'd left my house.

He had also left a dozen text messages. It would be quicker just to call him.

"Jeez, David, you couldn't call my house?" I muttered, as I pushed number two on my speed dial.

David picked up on the first ring.

"Alana, George Ferguson passed away."

David spoke in the full sentences he reserves for serious moments.

"No. Oh, no."

I found myself holding my breath as if, just maybe, it wasn't true.

"Yes. I just heard from Grace. She's devastated."

"The cops need to get on this!" I said angrily. "They're wasting time—"

"They know who did it. They lifted fingerprints off that sword. They're looking for Jenny Shu."

"Who's that?"

"One of our holiday hires."

I heard the horror in David's voice. I could only imagine how he felt.

"Oh, no," I said again. I tried to remember what Jenny Shu looked like. I remembered something about a little Asian girl fixing Lloyd's computer woes. "Do they know why she did it?"

"No. They are still looking for her. She is on the loose, so be careful out there. Where are you?"

"I'm delivering the last of Francis's letters. I'll be quick. What can we do for Grace?"

David didn't answer right away. I heard quiet voices in the background.

"Meredith and I are finishing up at Errands. We have to find someone to check out Lloyd's computer. Jenny was supposedly putting everything in order for him, but who knows what she did? Let's meet at Jorjana's. I'll call up there and see if her chef can put together a hot meal to take over to Grace's."

"Jorjana is dining in Santa Monica tonight," I said. "Get hold of Franklin and have him tell her the news. I don't want her to hear this over the phone."

"Will do, darling. See you at Jorjana's."

He made me promise to keep my phone in hand.

I slid to the passenger side, put the car in park, and turned off the ignition. The last thing in the world I felt like was a Happy Hour. I have to say, that was a first.

***

Pat Scott opened her front door with a welcoming smile.

One look at me put an end to that.

"Oh, dear, what's happened?"

"George Ferguson is dead," I said bluntly.

Pat paled. Standing on her doorstep, I gave her the details.

"Oh, dear," she repeated. "Come inside. We'll need something stronger than wine."

I followed her into her living room. Pat's home sat at the edge of a bluff. One wall of the room consisted of sliding glass doors that showcased the view. A door was open, and a breeze flowed in, filling the place with the scent of salt water. Pat's decorating sense leaned toward the eclectic. The furniture was well worn and the walls lined with bookcases. Artwork ranged from Indonesian masks, to Venetian glass sculptures, to those weird but colorful papier-mâché animals made in Mexico. I thought that if Pat explained how she obtained everything, I would have heard her life story.

We sat in front of the fireplace on a very cozy couch. I felt a thousand years old. Pat must have sensed this. She said, "Why don't you start at the beginning?"

So I did. I covered everything from my confronting Lloyd, to the race to the hospital, to the call from David.

It was hard to believe all of it had taken place within a few hours. While I talked, Pat retrieved a crystal decanter and a couple of glasses. The decanter held a Scotch of better-than-average blend. I couldn't drink it. I took a polite sip and put the glass down.

"This sword," Pat said. "Did it look like this?"

She pulled a book from the shelf next to her. The book was titled *Fundamental Kendo*. She opened it to a page and handed it to me. The page showed a photo of a man dressed in a long black robe and wearing something that looked like a hockey goalie's mask. In his hand was a sword described as a *shinai*.

"It did look a lot like this, but the handle was wrapped in duct tape."

"Hmm. Sounds like he damaged the *shinai* when he attacked you and Frannie," Pat said. "He must have used the duct tape to repair it."

"It wasn't a *he*," I said. "The police are looking for a young woman who worked at Errands, Etc."

"Oh, no."

That seemed to be the phrase of the day. We were quiet for a few moments. There just didn't seem to be anything to say.

"What a tragedy," Pat said. "Frannie never got the chance to tell George she was his mother, and George never got a chance to realize what she sacrificed for him. He wasted his life worshiping the ghost of Lydia Attel."

"That's another thing....George thought Lydia was still alive."

"Good heavens! Why?" Pat's mouth dropped right open.

"We'll never know, but George's girlfriend said he spent a lot of time trying to track down a death certificate and never found one."

"There must be a good explanation for that," Pat said. "Things were different—"

"Yeah, I know. Things were different then," I said none too nicely. I was sick of hearing about it.

But then it occurred to me that by accepting that things were different then, we were missing a piece of the story.

"We're overlooking something," I said. "First, babies are dealt out like a deck of cards, and no one bothered to officially record it. Now Lydia's death certificate is missing. Somehow this is all connected."

Pat cradled her glass and considered my comments.

"Whatever the connection is, I just can't see it," she finally said. "Do you have Frannie's letter? Maybe that will give us a clue."

I pulled the letter out of my bag and handed it to her. Unlike Dot and Celeste, Pat tore open the envelope without hesitation. She read the letter matter-of-factly, as if she were checking the paper for movies playing. When she was done, she handed it to me.

Dearest Pat,

It has been such a long time. I remember fondly our trips to Coronado. I regret having lost touch with my old friends, and I would like to reconnect with you and Celeste and Dot.

Our lives have taken such different paths. I always envied your having the courage to go back to school. But my life with Milton was rich in its own way. He is gone now, and I find myself daydreaming about the old days. Wouldn't it be fun to return to the Hotel del Coronado and drink a couple of Tom Collinses?

Alana Fox is delivering this letter for me because I am too much of a coward to face you myself. Please let Alana know if you are willing to take up again with an old friend.

Fondly,
Frannie

"Francis mentioned that she lacked courage in all three letters," I noted. "What was that about?"

"We used to tease her that she was afraid of her own shadow," Pat said. "But she was tougher than we gave her credit for. Milton was a very difficult man, and she put up with him all those years. That said, this doesn't give us any clues, does it?"

It didn't.

On that note I stood to leave. Pat walked me out to my car as we exchanged the usual niceties about giving her best to Grace and Mark and so on. I was rooting around in my bag for my car keys when Pat called out, "Meredith!"

It was dark out, but I recognized Meredith Mackenzie walking toward us. I remembered that she lived in Paradise Cove too. Pricey real estate, designer bags—she had done well for herself.

She looked young and hip again, and I would have hated her for it, but she also looked beaten down. For once in my life, I could empathize.

"Hi, Pat. Hi, Alana." Meredith even sounded dispirited.

"How are you holding up?" I asked. "David told me about your employee. What's her name again?"

"Jenny Shu. But her real name is Kiwako Ito." Meredith sensed my interest and went on. "David was having problems getting her bonded, which makes sense now. She gave him a false name and social security number. Turns out she has warrants in Fresno. She broke into the offices of the Archdiocese there and attempted to steal some kind of records. She beat up a security guard, but she was arrested then released on bail. Then she skipped town."

Meredith seemed relieved to get this all off her chest.

"Did you have any idea she was capable of this?" I asked.

"No. She seemed like a nice, hardworking kid. Apparently all this happened recently. The cops said she has a child who's really sick and needs a transplant. Her family thinks she went off the deep—"

Pat Scott gasped.

Meredith and I turned toward her.

I, for one, had forgotten Pat was there.

"Her name is Ito? Is this girl of Japanese descent?" Pat was pale.

"I guess so. She's Asian of some sort," Meredith said. "Why?"

Pat turned to me. "Alana, didn't you say George was convinced that Lydia was still alive?"

"That's what his girlfriend said, yeah."

"What did Lloyd say to that?"

I had to think. It seemed so long ago.

"He seemed surprised."

"But he didn't deny it?"

"No."

"That's the connection we couldn't see!" Pat cried. "Lydia really is still alive, and Kiwako is looking for her!"

"*What?*"

Meredith and me. In unison no less.

"Lloyd told you that Lydia's baby was sent to Fresno to be adopted out of a convent there. The Archdiocese of Fresno would have the records of that adoption. That's what Kiwako was looking for when she broke into the offices," Pat explained. "This Kiwako Ito must be Lydia Attel's granddaughter."

"How can that be?" I asked. "Lydia had an affair with her gardener."

My mind went back to the Mexican laborers around Celeste's pool. And around every other pool in California.

Pat knew what I was thinking. "In the forties most gardeners in Los Angeles were Japanese."

Chapter Twenty-Nine

"Lydia's gardener was Japanese?"

Me, herding cats while blindfolded again.

"Yes. The Japanese settled in Southern California before the war. Like most immigrants, they took on manual-labor jobs," Pat said. "The attending nurse overheard an argument between Mr. Attel and Milton. He was mad at Milton for letting the gardener come back to work after he returned from internment. Apparently there had been some nonsense going on between Lydia and the young man at the beginning of the war."

"Why do you think Jenny is looking for Lydia?" I asked.

"Because her child needs a transplant!" Pat cried out, as if that were the most obvious fact imaginable.

Meredith and I just stared at her.

"Children of Japanese-Caucasian descent have a particularly difficult time finding donor matches," Pat explained, as if tutoring a class of nursing students.

"Jenny must be looking for Lydia because she's a blood relative and might be a match for the sick child. It makes perfect sense. The Archdiocese had the records of the original adoption."

"Why wouldn't she just ask the Archdiocese for the records?" Meredith asked.

"Adoptions were sealed," Pat said. "It would be impossible to get them to open those records. That's why she broke into the offices. She was looking for a blood relative for a donor."

"She must have found the adoption records," I said. "She got Milton's name, and that brought her to Malibu."

"And she got a job that would give her information on just about every household in town," Meredith pointed out grimly. "Except Francis Ferguson's. How did she get in her house?"

"She broke in. That's why the cops thought it was a burglary." I was guessing now, but it made sense. "Jenny broke into the house Milton used to live in. That's why the jewelry wasn't stolen. She was looking for information on Lydia."

"How does George figure into this?" Meredith asked.

That's when all the little cats I had trouble herding in my head started to line up nice and straight. The key was something that George's girlfriend had said.

"George was searching online for Lydia's death certificate," I said. "His girlfriend said he never found it, and then he started hanging out in chat rooms. He and Jenny must have connected there. When Jenny got Milton's name, she also got Lydia's. George and Jenny were looking for the same person."

"That makes sense," Meredith said. "If there's anything Jenny knows about, it's computer stuff. But why would she kill him? It sounds like they had the same goal."

"My guess is she's desperate by now," Pat said. "She has a seriously ill child, and time may be running out. If George didn't give her the answers she wanted, she must have tried to beat it out of him. Poor, poor man. I pray the police catch her before anyone else gets hurt. But I'm sure she's long gone by now."

"No, she's not. She came into work today," Meredith said. "I saw her just this afternoon."

"Why on earth would she stick around Malibu?" Pat asked.

"Because she didn't find what she's looking for, and she won't stop until she does," I said, as the final little cat took its place in the line. "There's one person whose nose is in every corner of this business. If anyone knows if Lydia is alive it's—"

"Lloyd!" Meredith gasped. "Jenny was restoring his computer system after the storm. Lloyd was really upset when he realized she had access to all of his personal information."

"And Lloyd didn't deny that Lydia was still alive," I said. "If Jenny didn't find what she was looking for in his computer files, she may go after him next!"

Meredith was on it. She punched a number into her cell. She didn't like what she saw. "This is Lloyd's emergency number. He *always* answers it. He's not answering."

"I'm sure there's a good explanation," I said.

I didn't believe that for a nanosecond.

***

Meredith drove my car. Not that I had any say in it. She grabbed the keys from me and told me to get in. She pealed out of Paradise Cove and had us barreling down PCH like she was driving the Indy 500.

"Try calling David," she told me. "He was still at the office when I left. He can check on Lloyd."

"David's not answering," I said after dialing.

Meredith glanced at her watch.

"That's not like him," I told her. "He stays glued to that phone of his until midnight every night."

"I'm sure there's a good explanation," she said, which I didn't believe.

Meredith got us to the Town Center in just under no time at all. David's little red sports car and Lloyd's Mercedes were the only vehicles in the parking lot. That made sense, since the businesses were closed for the day. If I didn't have a wrenching twist in my gut, I would have thought all was normal.

Then my cell phone vibrated. I forgot I still had it in my hand.

"Hey! I just got a text from David!" I said with relief.

The relief dropped away the second I read the text.

Help. Lloyd office.

Meredith pulled her gun and a flashlight out of her tote bag. She gave me the flashlight.

"Follow me," she said.

We raced past Beans and flew up the stairs. I kept close behind her, illuminating the way as best I could. The door to Lloyd's office lay wide open.

Meredith went in first.

The lights in the reception area were off. To the left of the front desk, a frosted-glass door guarded the hallway that led to Lloyd's private office. A light shone at the end of the hallway. Meredith tried the door handle. Locked.

We heard voices coming from Lloyd's office.

"Tell me!" a woman yelled.

Then came a sickening clap. Then a moan.

Another clap. Another moan.

Meredith put her fingers to her lips and stepped behind the receptionist desk. She pointed at a bookcase. I focused the light up, and she reached for a set of books—a false set of books, as it turned out. The books swung open to reveal a switch. Meredith flipped the switch, and the bookcase swung open.

The fact that Lloyd had a secret entrance to his office surprised me. The fact that Meredith knew about it did not.

A hidden corridor ran parallel to the one that led to Lloyd's office. Meredith sprinted down it, with me close on her heels. At the end Meredith peered through what looked like a window. I realized we stood behind Lloyd's really ugly postmodern painting. The painting was actually a front to secretly view the proceedings in his office.

Lloyd sat with his back to us. His hands were tied with bungee cords to the stainless-steel arms of one of his low-slung chairs. His head slumped forward.

David lay on the floor facing us. He was curled up in a fetal position. There was a welt on his forehead, and one eye was swollen shut. At first glance I thought he was unconscious. But then I saw that he cradled his cell phone and was texting furiously. My phone vibrated like crazy in my hand.

Jenny Shu/Kiwako Ito stood over Lloyd. She held the *shinai* like she knew what she was doing. "Where is she?" she demanded. "Where is Lydia Attel?" With her free hand, she grabbed Lloyd by the hair and jerked his head back.

"On the count of three," Meredith whispered to me.

On the count of three, what? I had no idea what she was talking about.

Meredith picked up one of her long legs and slammed it against the wall. The wall swung open into the room. Meredith rushed forward.

I followed her because she had the gun.

Jenny jumped away from Lloyd and raised her arms above her head. She held the *shinai* in her hands. She turned to one side and swung. The sword resounded with a nasty whip through the air. Meredith ducked just in time and tackled Jenny full on. They both fell to the floor. The gun dropped from Meredith's hands and skittered across the floor.

Meredith had the advantage of size and weight, but Jenny came out of the fall on top of her. She brought one knee down hard on Meredith's stomach. A whoosh of air escaped Meredith's mouth. Jenny raised the sword.

She took aim at Meredith's head.

And then *bang*!

I shot Jenny with Meredith's gun.

Left-handed, no less.

Chapter Thirty

"Was it not a lovely service?" Jorjana asked.

"Yes, it was," I agreed. "You were wonderful to hold the reception here."

Jorjana and I sat in the larger of the two York reception halls. We had just returned from the combined memorial service for Francis and George. Family and friends mingled quietly around a buffet table set with the best the York staff could offer. By any measure, it was a generous feast of cold roast beef, smoked salmon, and salads, with coffee and desserts at a separate table. There would be no invoice to settle at the end of the day. Jorjana was like that.

It had been a lovely service indeed, with lots of flowers and organ music and a minister who somehow knew just what to say. But it had been heartbreaking as well. No matter how many psalms were sung or prayers said, the fact that a mother and son had died senselessly did not go away. It would take time for Grace and Mark and their families to heal from these tragedies.

And they still had to endure the trial of Kiwako Ito.

It turns out that I'm a lousy shot. I didn't kill Jenny/Kiwako; I only managed to mangle her shoulder. Poetic justice in some small manner. After the surgery to remove the bullet, she was sent straight to jail. With any luck she never would get out again.

"Darlings, there you are." David lowered himself into a chair next to us. The welt on his forehead was less pronounced. He wore a black eye patch over his injured eye. Privately both Jorjana and I thought he might keep the thing permanently as a swashbuckling accessory.

David and Lloyd had been caught by surprise when Jenny/Kiwako burst into the office demanding to know the whereabouts of Lydia Attel. David had tried a rugby move to stop her but hadn't figured on her skill with the *shinai*. She, in turn, hadn't figured on his prowess of texting with one hand.

"Jorjana, darling, the minister just arrived and would like a word," David said.

"Certainly." Jorjana straightened in her chair and put on her gracious-hostess face. "Alana, will you join us?"

"You two go ahead," I said. "I'll grab a bite to eat."

David pushed Jorjana's wheelchair through the crowd. They passed Grace and Mark, who were accepting condolences by the fireplace and holding up as well as could be expected. Meredith had hired a whole new set of employees just to take care of their families for the next few weeks. There would be no invoice for that either.

Turned out Meredith is like that too.

"Alana!"

Pat Scott stood at the dessert table flanked by Dot and Celeste. Pat and Celeste were dressed appropriately in black, and Dot was dressed like Dot. A scent of mothballs made me suspect Dot had dipped into one of the trunks in her magic vault.

"Lydia is alive after all?" Pat asked after we exchanged hellos.

I had tried to keep the ladies updated over the past few days, but it had been like, well, trying to herd cats. Her family in Fresno explained the horrible story of Jenny/Kiwako. Jenny did have a daughter in need of a bone marrow transplant. The family had tested every member looking for a match but came up empty. That's when Jenny started researching her grandfather's biological family. Her request to view the adoption records was rejected by the Archdiocese of Fresno. As her daughter became sicker, Jenny grew desperate. After breaking into the Archdiocese offices, she found the information that led her to the Ferguson clan.

"Yes, Lydia is in a private nursing facility in Ojai," I said. "She's been there almost sixty years. That story about tuberculosis was made up after Lydia nearly scalded George in the tub. Douglas Attel and Milton were afraid of what she might do, so they had her committed there and made up the story to spare the family. They went as far as staging a funeral for her."

"How is she?" Pat asked.

"She's ninety, blind, arthritic, and suffering from dementia," I said. "She's in no shape to donate bone marrow."

"So the child is still in need of a donor," Pat noted. "What a waste. What a horrible, horrible waste."

"Even all these years later, Lydia is causing heartbreak," said Celeste.

"What about Lloyd?" Dot asked. "Is he sorry yet?"

Celeste and Pat tried to shush her. I have to say, I admired Dot's bluntness. If anyone had listened to Dot back in the day and stayed far away from Milton, they would have all been spared a lot of grief.

"Lloyd is still in the hospital, but he'll recover," I said. "He sustained a pretty bad head injury, and a man his age doesn't bounce back so quickly. But he is heartsick, as you might imagine. He wanted you all to know that even though Lydia is still alive, Milton and Francis were legally married. Douglas Attel pulled the strings to have the marriage between Milton and Lydia annulled."

I knew they would find that interesting. I wasn't prepared for how relieved they all looked. Really, after all that had happened?

"We have something to tell you too, Alana." Pat gave a wan smile. "Good news, actually. Go ahead, Dot. Tell her."

"We're all goin' to go to the Hotel del Coronado," Dot began. "We agreed that it's time to forgive Frannie. We're gonna sit on the veranda and drink Tom Collinses and toast Frannie's memory. But that's not all. We decided we're too young to sit around on verandas all day. We're gonna take that money I got from Milton and start up a magic school just for girls. Whaddya think?"

I thought it was wonderful, and I told them so. I refrained from suggesting they could rent a space from Lloyd. But you can bet your life, the second that man got out of the hospital, I was going to demand he give them a place gratis.

Meredith Mackenzie wandered in just then. I excused myself to chat with her.

"Is Lloyd's office back in order?" I asked.

The cleanup had been ugly. Jenny/Kiwako had first tried to intimidate Lloyd and David by breaking everything she could with the *shinai*. Books were torn off the shelves. The photos of Lloyd fishing were shattered. When that tactic didn't produce results, she turned the sword on then.

To Lloyd's credit, he never did divulge Lydia's whereabouts to Jenny/Kiwako. It nearly cost him his life. Only when he learned of her arrest, did he share the secret with Grace and Mark. They told David, who then told everyone who would listen. David would dine out on the story and his eye patch for months.

Meredith and I took it upon ourselves to see that order was restored to Lloyd's office. We ordered new carpet. We hired painters. We had the pictures reframed. And then, while we were putting the things back on the bookshelves, we found Lloyd's Rolodex mixed in with his fishing reels.

The Rolodex contained the address of the hospital that cared for Lydia along with all the contact information for the players involved in the adoption of Lydia's baby. On her first day of working for Lloyd, Jenny/Kiwako sat less than three feet away from the information she sought desperately for in Lloyd's computer files. If she had known what a Rolodex was,

Francis and George might still be alive. Suffice it to say, Meredith and I would share that awful realization forever.

"Everything looks good in the office," Meredith said. "David showed me your new space. He did such a good job there that I'm taking him with me to Pottery Barn."

"Are you remodeling your office, too?" I asked.

"No, I'm decorating my *home*," Meredith said. "You know how they say your life flashes before your eyes when you die? Well, I thought I was going to die when Jenny pinned me down, and at that moment, I regretted never having made a home for myself. First thing tomorrow, David and I are going shopping."

"Second thing tomorrow," I corrected her. "David has to follow up with my insurance agent first."

"I'll be sure to remind him!" Meredith said. "Are you working tomorrow?"

"I think I'll stay home and catch up."

The catching up I had ahead of me made my head spin. Thanksgiving was three days away. I had invitations to sort through; clients to contact, and a five-year business plan to go over with a fine-tooth comb.

And I needed to get my hands on Stan Sanchez. I had something important to discuss with him.

As if on cue, Stan walked into the room. Even if I hadn't seen him, I would have known he was there. Every woman with a pulse stopped talking and stared.

Stan wore a suit that fit him just badly enough to be adorable. His tie was slightly askew; his arm was in a cast; and he was far and away the most handsome man I'd ever laid eyes on.

I excused myself from Meredith and went to him.

"Hey, there." Stan greeted me with a kiss. All the women in the room shot me a dirty look.

"Hey, there yourself," I said.

"Nice turnout." Stan's gaze took in the room. "How was the service?"

"Lovely. Exhausting. Are you hungry?"

Stan looked over to the buffet and shook his head.

"Good. Let's go up to my suite. I have something to say to you."

Stan's eyes lit up.

"And I have a perfectly chilled Champagne to say it with."

"Champagne?" Stan said in surprise. "It's only eleven in the morning!"

I took him by the tie and led him away.

"It's five o'clock somewhere."

NOTES

On my desk I have a framed quote from the author C.W. Grafton. It reads, "I know it is true. I made it up myself."

'The Third Side' is a work of fiction- at least the plot is. Most of the characters are fictional- a product of my over active imagination. The Malibu Town Center was made up to suit the purposes of the story- if it were real it would sit right on top of Legacy Park. The Beach Shack is based on The Beach Café at Paradise Cove but the Beach Shack has a bigger, darker bar- the clam chowder is excellent in both places.

The Food Whores dining group is actually a regular gathering of women friends of mine in Seattle. Becky Selengut is a real person too; a talented chef who puts up with the antics of the Whores every other month or so.

The ideas for this story came from two sources. Years after my beloved mother-in-law passed away, my husband discovered her adoption papers hidden within the frame of an old photo of his mother and her parents. This came as a total shock to everyone and we suspect she would have been surprised herself. This planted the 'times were different then' aspect to the story. The second idea was born from a news story about a child of Caucasian-Asian descent in desperate need of a bone marrow transplant and the difficulty the family had in finding a donor.

I set my stories in Malibu because I fell in love with the place more than twenty years ago. When our Darling Son was a toddler he and I spent days on end at the beaches digging sand castles and watching the pelicans dive for fish. The thrill of seeing dolphins up close and the annoyance of really aggressive sea gulls is not something you forget soon. And then there is the splendid wilderness that is Malibu-the changing color of the ocean, the scent of the sage, the quiet of the morning fog. That wonder seeped into my soul.

Time and circumstances have led me away physically but in my heart I never left.

Malibu is a state of mind. Once you get it, you never forget it.

ABOUT THE AUTHOR

M. A. Simonetti is a graduate of the Mystery Writing Program at the University of Washington.

As a "Woman of a Certain Age," Simonetti recognizes the lack of heroines in popular fiction that are women over age forty. She is doing her damndest to provide a broader representation.

The author divides her time between the heavy traffic of Southern California and the heavy rain of the Pacific North Wet.